MURDER AND DECEPTION

Warren C. Holloway

GOOD 2 GO PUBLISHING

MURDER AND DECEPTION
Written by Warren C. Holloway
Cover Design: Davida Baldwin, Odd Ball Designs
Typesetter: Mychea
ISBN: 9781947340770

Published 2022 by Good2Go Publishing
7311 W. Glass Lane • Laveen, AZ 85339
www.good2gopublishing.com
https://twitter.com/good2gobooks
G2G@good2gopublishing.com
www.facebook.com/good2gopublishing
www.instagram.com/good2gopublishing

MURDER AND DECEPTION
Written by Warren C. Holloway
Cover Design: Davida Baldwin, Odd Ball Designs
Typesetter: Mychea
ISBN: 9781947340770

Published 2022 by Good2Go Publishing
7311 W. Glass Lane • Laveen, AZ 85339
www.good2gopublishing.com
https://twitter.com/good2gobooks
G2G@good2gopublishing.com
www.facebook.com/good2gopublishing
www.instagram.com/good2gopublishing

ONE

Present Day, 9:03 PM
Harrisburg, Pennsylvania

"911, what's your emergency?"

"Help me! Oh my God! Somebody is in my house!" the shaken female screamed through the phone in fear.

"Who is in your house, ma'am?" the female dispatcher questioned, locating her address via computer, tracing the call in order to send officers to her home.

"I don't know. I heard the glass breaking followed by a male's voice coming up the steps. Please help me. He's going to hurt my baby boy." She broke down crying, having terrifying thoughts of how this was all going to play out.

"What's your name?"

"Brandi."

"Okay, Brandi, I have units coming to your residence now. Stay on the line. Where are you in the house?"

"I'm in my bedroom. My son is in his room," she responded in a tremulous tone.

"Lock your bedroom door," she suggested, not thinking the intruder would be of any harm to her son, however, coming to burglarize the home.

"Okay, I'm locking it now," she replied, rushing over to the door and securing it. Her fear-filled, heavy breathing could be heard coming through the phone as tears streamed down her face. Her heart was beating just as fast as her breathing. Then it happened. A loud jolting banging came across the bedroom door she had just locked. Fear shot through her body, making her legs weak as she dropped to the floor, still clinging to the phone to her ear.

"Open the door now, or I'll kick this muthafucka in!" the aggressive male voice yelled from the other side.

"Could it be an ex-lover, or a crazed burglar?" she, along with the 911 dispatcher, was thinking, hearing the booming voice.

"Please leave my house. I don't have anything in here for you!" she said, still shaken, wanting help now. At the same time, she pulled herself away from the door while speaking in a low tone to the dispatcher. "Please help me. I don't want anything to happen to me or my son."

Brandi, now tuning into the Asounds on the other side of the door, could hear the creak of her son's bedroom door opening. She wanted to get it fixed a while back, but it also alerted her to when her son would get up in the middle of the night to use the bathroom. "I think he's in my son's room," she whispered to the dispatcher.

The 911 operator felt the intensity of what was taking place, also having young children of her own, knowing how she would feel being placed in such a horrific situation. She, too, would be in great distress having a stranger in her home, posing a threat to all she loved. "Brandi, I'm showing the police are closing in on your home. Can you hear the sirens?"

"Yes, I hear them coming now."

"Okay, I'll stay on the line with you until the officers come to get you," she said, wanting to comfort her as much as possible.

"Thank you. I just hope many son is okay. I should have run in his room first, before locking the door," she said, feeling guilty about having been overwhelmed by her fear.

The dispatcher, not wanting Brandi to beat herself up about this, tried to console her. "It's just fine. He's probably sound asleep. I know my boys would sleep through fireworks, but as soon as you mention new video games, they're wide awake." Her words brought a brief smirk to Brandi's face, knowing her son also loves the video games. "Brandi, is he still inside your home?"

"It's quiet. I don't know," she responded, staring at the door, like he was still standing on the other side in silence waiting for her to open it. She climbed to her feet as she heard the sirens pulling up in front of her house, accompanied by the red-and-blue lights bouncing off her house and surrounding homes. She parted the curtains and looked out to see three police cruisers, officers on the outside of the cars with guns out, looking up at the house, approaching.

One of the officers noticed her standing in the window. "Ma'am, is there anyone still in the home?" the officer yelled up. Her window was open, allowing the spring breeze to come through, so she could hear him clearly.

"I don't know. I'm not opening the bedroom door until you come up here, because he might be on the other side," she responded, glancing over her shoulder at the bedroom door, hoping they caught whoever was on the other side. Officer Jefferson, a forty-three-year-old Afro-American stood five foot eleven, with close black hair, a goatee, and a gap between his teeth that added to his character, something he always said. He'd been on the force seven years now. Today he was the first on the scene, never having a situation where the victim was stuck inside the home with the potential suspected burglar. Not good, because it could easily turn into a hostage situation if he was still present. "Hey, guys, I need one of you men to guard the front door. Also keep eyes on her. The other can follow me so we can take the back in case they try to run out," Officer

Jefferson said, knowing most home burglaries occur through back doors and windows.

They took their flashlights out, heading through the alleyway with caution, ready for any sudden movements in the dark. They closed in on the back door. Each of them remained quiet as they proceeded, noticing the broken glass on the back door's window, the point of entry.

Guns out, they continued into the kitchen, coming to a halt when Officer Jefferson felt a crackling under his feet from his 230-pound frame crushing it. He flashed the light down and saw it was from a light bulb that was knocked out. "Why?" he wondered, it didn't make sense. They continued through the house into the plush living room and dining room, with a black, gold, and red theme, along with China sets in a lit cabinet. The black tiger statues on each side of the couch boasted gold stripes.

Once they cleared the downstairs, they made their way up the steps. In midstep they heard a loud thud, startling both officers. Skip, who had been on the force for close to a year now, expressed his thoughts on the sound: "I swear if you weren't in front of me, sir, I would have fired."

He looked over his shoulder at the rookie. "You shoot me by accident or not, you better kill me, 'cause I'll put a bullet in your ass to show you how that shit feels," he responded before proceeding up the steps and clearing the back room then the bathroom before popping into the middle room, a child's room, which looked like a crime scene. The Spiderman bed sheets seemed to be covered in blood, along with a blood trail that greeted them at the room entrance, where the blood trail ended, almost like they covered up the source of blood.

The sight of this has made each of their heart rates spike, knowing this breaking and entry had just shifted to a more serious offense. "This is not good, sir," Skip said in a low tone, eyes still glued to the trail of blood, fearing the worst for the child whose room this was. Skip, a young twenty-five-year-old, stood five foot nine, with fresh hair cut close, still having his baby face and baby-blue eyes.

"We need to get the mother out of her room to see if her son made it in there with her,"

Officer Jefferson said, not wanting a child to be involved in this crime. He came up on the bedroom door and tapped lightly. “Harrisburg Police, this is Officer Jefferson. Ma’am, it’s okay to open the door now.”

Brandi came to the door listening in, still shaken and hesitating to open the door. Then she heard his radio with other officers talking back and forth, communicating on other events. She opened the door and embraced the officer like a long-lost family member. “I’m glad you’re here; I’m so scared. I couldn’t get to my son in time. Is he still sleeping?” she questioned, releasing her embrace and looking past the officer toward her son’s room.

Brandi’s hazel-brown eyes filled with tears and fear, sensing something was wrong. The five-foot-five brown-skinned beauty normally had a radiant smile that glowed in a room of those paying attention to her. Her long black hair, even now, flowed effortlessly. She only weighed a hundred and twenty pounds, with her curves strategically placed. “What’s wrong, Officers? Where is my son?” she questioned, seeing the look on both of their faces.

Instinctively she pushed past them, rushing to her son's room. As soon as she came to the door, she followed the trail and came to a fear-filled halt, freezing her where she stood. Her eyes widened. Her mouth opened just as wide in disbelief. She sucked in a heated breath, only to let out, "Noooo, nooo, he took my baby boy!"

Officer Jefferson nodded to Skip to radio this in to Homicide so they could come out to investigate this burglary turned possible homicide. At the same time, Officer Jefferson knew to remove her from the crime scene so nothing was moved or touched, with her being deeply pained by this act against her son. They also needed to get information on her son and the time of events that unfolded before they got the call.

He took her downstairs to the living room, and Officer Skip got her some water from the kitchen before they questioned her. "What's your son's name and age?" Officer Jefferson asked with his notebook out ready to jot it all down.

She sipped her water before responding. "Nicholas Jackson. He's eight years old. That's him right there in the picture," she said, pointing to the photo on the end table by the lamp. Officer Jefferson took hold of the picture and looked on at the kid, thinking, who could do such a thing?

"That's my baby boy," she said, being a proud mom.

He placed the picture down to get back to questions. "When you heard the sound of someone in your home, where were you in the house? If you can run me through this, it would give me a visual for my report."

"I was watching TV with the volume low enough to hear if he got up or called for me. The show I was watching had just started when I heard the glass breaking, so I sat up quick. I didn't get out of bed right away, until I heard a man's voice coming up the steps. I jumped out of bed. I wanted to run to my son's room, but I was overwhelmed by fear, forcing me to react against my motherly instincts. I called 911 instead."

"You did the right thing calling us. Don't blame yourself. Did you see who was in your house?"

"No, but he sounded angry, banging on my door. Good thing the dispatcher told me to shut and lock the door," she responded, folding her arms, hugging herself for comfort.

"Who would want to bring harm to you or your son?"

"No one. I'm a school teacher at the high school."

"Is Nicholas's father around?"

"He's in jail right now but will be getting out soon."

"What's his name?" he asked, wanting to cover all ground.

"Ricky Smith."

"Ms. Jackson, there's a lot of blood in your son's room, as you've witnessed. At any time, did you hear him scream or call out to you?"

She stared up the steps as if to process her thoughts, visualizing the moment it all happened. "No, or maybe I did. I don't recall. I was so hysterical and scared. My screaming may have overshadowed it all. I should have run to his room. We could have been locked in there together."

"It's not your fault, ma'am. This scum should have never been in your home."

"Sir, the homicide crew just pulled up," Officer Skip said, looking out the window, seeing the unmarked Crown Victoria.

Two homicide detectives exited the car, making their way into the house, seeing all the nosey neighbors standing around to see what was going on. When the detectives entered the house, Officer Jefferson stood to greet them. "Harrisburg's finest, Tores and Anderson, how the hell are ya?"

"We'll be better once we figure out what's going on here," Detective Anderson said. JR Anderson was a Harrisburg native with street smarts. He had nine years on Homicide, solving 90 percent of his cases. The dark-skinned brother stood six foot even, was well groomed, and was a fit two hundred pounds. He was clean-shaven with a bald head, brown eyes, and a strong jawline, adding to his features. Serious when needed, he was a real charmer to the ladies . . .

TWO

"Detective Anderson, we have an unlawful entry and a kidnapping that left behind a trail of blood in the son's bedroom. I did a follow-up with questions, if you want to take a look at my notes," Officer Jefferson said.

"You said unlawful entry? Would this be the back door?" detective Janelle Tires questioned, not seeing anything wrong with the front door. Janelle, a Puerto Rican beauty standing five foot three, was a force to be reckoned with in this homicide field, having a keen eye that allowed her to pick things apart. The Latina had a smile of innocence coupled with dimples, adding to her luring sex appeal. Her light brown eyes glowed under the lights just as her smooth skin and flowing silky black hair, which she kept pulled back when she was working. She wore no makeup other than lip gloss, showing her true beauty, while having the intellect to accompany it.

"Yes, the back door is the way Officer Skip and I entered, noticing the breach."

"Then my partner and I will start at the back door and work our way upstairs," Detective Tores said.

"After we're done, we'll more than likely have questions for Ms. Jackson, to further assess this crime scene. Officer Jefferson, get a current photo of the kid and put an alert out for him," Detective Anderson said.

"I'm on it," he responded as they turned to head toward the back door.

Tores hit the light switch to no avail, so she removed her small flashlight and illuminated the kitchen, noticing the broken glass at the back door along with the shattered light bulb. "We need to have the back door printed," she said, flashing the light on it.

"It doesn't seem random to me, especially with the kid being taken. The burglar would wait until no one was home. A kidnapper would move undetected," Detective Anderson stated, processing the scene.

Tores looked over at him, taking in his theory. "It could be someone close to her. The boy's father, a jealous ex, family, or a deranged friend," she tossed her thoughts out there.

After processing the kitchen, they made their way upstairs. They both took in the amount of blood on the bed, followed by the trail of blood that ended at the door. They looked at each other, sensing something off or gone terribly wrong, meaning her son must've been killed. However, they needed more evidence to come to a conclusion.

"Officer Jefferson, can you have Ms. Jackson come up here please?" Detective Tores asked. Brandi came up the stairs still hugging herself, looking shocked and worried all at once, and rightfully so. "Can you run us through what took place up until these officers came to your home?" Detective Tores asked.

She did just that, recalling every detail as if watching a nightmarish movie with her and her son being the lead characters. The tears in her eyes were all too real, something Detective Tores took notice of before they excused her, allowing her to go back down to the living room while they did their detective work. Detective

Tores, also a single mother of a young three-year-old boy, had to push her emotions to the side, having a child involved in this case. However she would do her best in closing this case to find out who was responsible for this crime, whether it was a homicide or kidnapping. Whoever did this was callous yet calculated.

Detective Anderson didn't feel this was a random case. Having this in the back of his mind drove him to find out more. He even looked at things he normally wouldn't at a crime scene to get a sense of direction.

"It's a good bit of blood that suddenly stops at the door," Tores said. "They must not have been in a hurry to make sure the blood trail stopped."

He paused, looking at the blood spatter, then back to the bed. Something stood out to him with the blood spill pattern. The amount of blood on the bed suggested a brutal crime took place, which would leave a thicker blood trail even if it halted at the door to cover it up. "Was there more than one person involved here?" He wondered.

"I wouldn't exclude that there were two people and not just a lone suspect in this crime."

"You're thinking it was planned too?" she responded, then added, "The kid must have been struck to bring calm and control before covering him up."

"I know this city isn't going to let something like this fly. The mothers will take to social media creating chaos that warrants resolve to find this suspected kidnapper and child killer if this kid met his demise," Detective Anderson said, knowing what's ahead of him and his partner, taking on a case like this.

"She said she heard him talking on the way up the steps but couldn't make out what he was saying. This could mean he was communicating with someone else," Detective Tores stated.

"If he was talking to himself he would be crazy, and it explains this level of abrupt intrusion," Detective Anderson added, agreeing with his partner's assessment.

"We also need to check her financial background, see if she came into money or owed money. This would allow us to cross out the ransom for her son and focus more on the why and who would do this," Detective Tores said, knowing it was about to be sleepless nights until they closed this case, but she was up for the challenge, especially being a mother, wanting the same if this happened to her . . .

THREE

9:01 AM

The next morning, the detectives made their way to Camp Hill, Pennsylvania, less than five minutes from the city, crossing the I-83B bridge. They made their way to the super-maximum CDCC (Central Diagnostic Control Center), a state prison where Rick Smith was being held. This is the same place where five thousand plus notorious drug kingpins, serial killers, and rapist were secured behind the four fences, with cameras and eight guard towers, covering every inch of this level 4 and 5 facility.

Ricky was brought into the security office escorted by two guards, since he wasn't cuffed. He noticed the two detectives when he entered the room. "Have a seat, Mr. Smith," Detective Tores said, wanting to get right to it.

"What's this about? Y'all trying to keep me locked down knowing I'm about to get out?" he asked, with his face balled up.

"It depends on what we discover today," she responded.

Ricky stood five foot eleven, with curly hair on top with a bald fade on the side. He had a light mustache, and the rest of his face was clean shaven. He was only thirty years old and looked young, having stayed fit by lifting weights over the years.

"Mr. Smith, you may know about your son since inmates keep their ears to the streets?" Detective Anderson questioned, to check his demeanor.

Ricky's eyes cut sharp toward JR. "What happen to my son?" Ricky snapped, until the guards stepped closer, reminding him of their presence.

"As of last night he became missing, and from the looks of things, there seems to be foul play. That brings us here, to tie up all suspect possibilities." Ricky's entire demeanor shifted, along with the smirk on his face.

"You think this shit is funny, or did I say something to amuse you?" Detective Anderson snapped, leaning forward, staring intently at Ricky, close to coming over the table. "We can hold your parole up if this investigation of your missing son entertains you that much."

"My smirk is because Brandi is crazy to have you thinking I would bring harm to my son."

"I don't know what you and her have going on, but our concern is your son," Detective Tores said.

"Why are you quick to blame her?" Detective Anderson asked.

"I'm not blaming her. I just said she's crazy. Outside of that, I love my son and would do anything for him."

"Even kidnap him if you can't have custody?" Detective Tores fired, trying to catch him off guard.

"You're wasting time with these antics. I will tell you this, if someone outside of her brought harm to my son, they will pay. You know who I am; otherwise, you wouldn't be here."

"We don't need to add violence to this situation. Let us do our job. We'll get to the bottom of this," she said.

"Don't get too comfortable with the thoughts of freedom, just in case we have to come back here with a different outcome pointing in your direction," Detective Anderson tossed out, wanting to stand firm closing the interview out.

Ricky just stared at the two of them, pissed they would come at him like this.

After the interview, they exited the prison, when a call came through on Tores's cell phone. "Detective Tores speaking."

"Detective, this is Officer Marshall. We have another missing kid situation. I know you're homicide. I just figured with the case last night, you may want to look into this for any connection."

"I'm interested. Give me your location," she said, intrigued to find out if there were any similar findings.

"1923 Brookwood Street. The kid is Ivan Robinson, age twelve, chubby little fella. The mother is Danika Estille."

"Thank you, Officer Marshal," she said, ending the call before relaying it to her partner. "We have another case to look into with a missing child." She gave off this smile that really expressed her fears of this case being linked to the one last night.

JR also picked up on the look, having seen it before. "You always have his look I think is beautiful, expressing other means behind the smile." He said, with her having good instincts that always helped closing cases thus far.

FOUR

Meanwhile, over in the city in someone's cold, damp basement, young Ivan Robinson was sitting secured to a chair with duct tape. His eyes were covered with a cloth, and his mouth was gagged. He was knocked unconscious in order to get him here quietly, safe and sound, so he could face what was to come. He was lured by his attacker before he was hit with a syringe filled with sedatives that rushed into his bloodstream, sending him into a world of darkness. Now he was awake, fully alert, yet not knowing where he was or how he got secured to this chair or blindfolded. He did feel the cold, damp air and the floor beneath his bare feet. Fear came over him as he started shaking, trying to break free, not wanting to be in this position. He heard about the other kid being kidnapped from his mom, who worried all the time. Now, he was the kidnapped child. Overwhelmed by thoughts of being violated, he pissed on himself, struggling to break free, all to no avail. He screamed out for his mom, muffled by the gag. She couldn't hear him even if his mouth wasn't secured. He was a long way from home. The silence in the basement didn't help much, with him hearing his own heart and heavy breathing. Suddenly, a television directly behind him blared out sound bites from different TV shows taunting Ivan, before the kidnapper came around to the front of him, staring intently with dark murderous eyes, ready to take Ivan's life.

"You've been quite the badass fat boy. Uh oh, you don't look so tough now, pissing all over yourself now, do you? Don't worry, because I'm going to beat the shit out of you. Ha ha ha, that's funny, right, fat boy?" they taunted him before stepping to his side, up close to his ear, breathing on him heavy, sending a bone-chilling tingling down his spine, making him squirm, trying to evade this person's presence. "You're going to pay feeling the pain, while I get a kick out of it." Right then they kicked Ivan violently in the face with force, sending him and the chair flipping on its side.

Another brute kick followed by more until blood sprayed from his face, coming from his nose, busted lips, and cuts above his eyes. They even started stomping his head, rupturing his eardrum, blood spewing from his ear. They halted the stomping and stepped back, breathing heavy as if working out. They wanted to take a look at the art of this blood-painted face.

"Look, you've made a mess," the person said, taking a plastic bag and covering his pulsating bloody head and face, sealing the bag around his neck, cutting off all much-needed oxygen, forcing Ivan to struggle and squirm for air and life.

He didn't have a chance with the bag being secured with duct tape, cutting off all oxygen. The kidnapper turned killer was now watching his body shake violently in attempt to get air while fighting off death, which has a stronghold on him, pulling him closer to the darkness of no more. His body came to a halt, and at the same time the killer exhaled, as if getting a rush out of murder, seeing one's life slip from their flesh. The killer washed all of Ivan's things before cleaning up, wanting everything to be perfect as they had planned it in their mind. Now they would have to dispose of his body, without leaving any traces that would point back to them. They couldn't have this; it would ruin everything, especially the fun and the rush that murder gives them. They also had to make sure they were on schedule with their daily life, not to look out of place. They knew the good detectives would be paying attention to every detail. They just had to stay ahead of them.

FIVE

11:31 AM

The detectives finally made their way to the Brookwood address to speak with Danika Estille in regards to her missing son Ivan Robinson. "Ms. Estille, you called reporting your son missing. Normally a child his age would be with his friends or at school this time of day," Detective Anderson said, trying to get a feel for what was going on.

"My son should be at school, but he's not. I got a call this morning saying he didn't show up. He has perfect attendance certificates and good grades and loves school. So as a mother, I sensed something must be wrong with my son."

"Who does your son hang around?" he asked, knowing that peer pressure could have made him skip school.

"The kids he normally hangs out with are all at school right now. This is how I know something is wrong. I just want my son to be okay and come home safe."

"Is that your son in the photo?" Detective Tores asked, noticing the kid in the picture in his football attire.

"That's him. He loves playing football," she responded, smiling at the image of her son in the picture, reflecting back to him playing at Sunshine Park with Coach Chism.

Detective Tores made her way over to the group of family photos with Ivan in it, taking it all in while trying to connect the dots between this case and the one last night.

"Do you have any relatives in the area where your son would feel comfortable going to, to skip school, or in case of an emergency?" Detective Anderson asked. "No, no, he's not with any of them. Trust me, Detective, I called around to everyone I know, friends and family, to make sure I don't look like a fool in calling 911 for a missing child, then he shows up. This is all too real for me, and I wish he was skipping school with his friends, but they're at school," she responded, clearly upset, not that it was the detective's intention. He just needed to cover all angles so he wouldn't be chasing a ghost trail of a crime that didn't take place.

Little did they all know, it was far too late for young Ivan Robinson. He was gone and wouldn't be found unless the killer decided it to be necessary or a part of their master plan and grand scheme, adding thrills to the rush of murder.

"Ms. Estille, I have a son, so I can relate to the level of concern you have being a mother. We will do all we can to find your son. Hopefully he's playing video games somewhere. Either way, we're on the job to make sure he comes home safe," Detective Tores said, nodding her head to JR, letting him know that they're done here.

"Here's my card, if he comes home before we find him. You can also call if something comes up and you need my partner and me to look into it," Detective Anderson said, standing up and handing her the card.

"Detectives, take this picture; it's his favorite. This is his million-dollar pose, he always says," Danika said, giving them the photo of him flexing his biceps.

They gave a brief smile, looking on at the picture accompanied by her words of his saying it's his million-dollar pose. "Thank you, ma'am. I hope we can bring some resolve and joy back into your life in bringing him home safe," Detective Tores said, placing a smile on Danika's face at the thought of her son walking through the door, the same door the detectives were exiting, heading back to the car.

Once inside the car, each of them sighed simultaneously, turning the XM Radio on and listening to soft R&B playing, relaxing them. "I don't like what I see taking place in our city, Janelle. This feeling isn't sitting right with me either."

Janelle turned the radio down as she drove off, ready to address this serious matter they were taking on. "We'll be fine as long as we apply ourselves, thinking as we always do to close all cases we take on."

"I don't fear much working this job, but what gets me is if we have a child kidnapper slash killer as it was in Atlanta in the '80s. The eyes of social media aren't going to help with that type of continuous pressure."

"Social media can also be our friend, helping us solve this case."

SIX

As the detectives headed to lunch, the killer was over at the disclosed location, wiping down the lifeless body of Ivan Robinson while reflecting back on the kill, the feeling it gave them. This act of false care was sadistic and perverted, getting thrills from this. The killer was paying close attention to being clean and meticulous, wanting everything to be and go as they had formed it in their unstable mind. They removed the duct tape and plastic bag, along with anything that wasn't natural. All bruises were cleaned and patched up as if they were to ever heal in death. Once the body was cleaned to their liking, they stood back, taking a photo for a souvenir, something they would look back on, to relive the very moment of murder. A smile formed on the killer's face, staring at his lifeless body as if it were a portrait. The art of murder even.

The killer spoke in a whisper, not wanting to be heard, it seemed, as if people were around. “Yes, you look so good now. Are you ready for your big media debut?” they said, knowing where they were about to take his body. Leaving it behind would get media attention, creating a frenzy, a distraction maybe, just as they wanted. After taking more pictures, they dressed him back in his freshly washed clothing, wanting him to look good, being in clean clothing. His shirt and pants were pressed. “It’s time to go, my friend. There are more just like you, dying to see me. Get it, dying to see me? No one will see me coming until it’s all over with. Then it’ll be too late. Yessss, just the way I want it,” the killer whispered, amused by their own dialogue. The killer felt they were smarter than those that came before them, because they knew how they got caught and what their mistakes were, making them sloppy. They didn’t plan on getting caught or slipping up as they had done. They also planned on keeping close tabs on the detectives leading the case. Therefore they could be many steps ahead of them, if or when they thought they were close.

The killer's main focus was to be in and out, to get what they came for, then, poof, vanish as if they never existed. In doing this, it would leave a cold trail of deception. The kidnapper/killer knew about the detectives and their high percentage of closing cases. Having this knowledge added even more excitement and fun to the chase, to this unwieldy situation.

"Detectives, I'm being naughty right now, and no one is here to catch me," the killer said staging the body where they chose. At the same time, they were in disguise, creating layers to this deception, in case cameras were placed on the homes or buildings around. "I'll leave Ivan's body right here with hopes you slowpokes catch up to me later to make it interesting. Okay, bye-bye," they said, slipping off calmly as if nothing was wrong with what they had just done. Even more crazy, no one was around to see this kid's body being placed there.

SEVEN

Back uptown at the Camp Curtin Barbecue Pit, the detectives were stuffing their faces, fueling up on lunch, with the savory barbecue pork ribs, hearty fries, barbecue chicks, greens, and baked macaroni, chasing it all down with lemonade. As they enjoyed their food, they went over the case.

"I have an idea," Detective Tores said, stuffing her mouth with hearty fries topped with shredded beef barbecue and hot melting cheese.

"The last time you had an idea, things got crazy, nothing turned out as we expected."

"Don't tell me you're still hanging onto the time when the murder suspect barricaded himself into the house? I didn't expect that to happen. Anyway, my idea is pulling the files on all the newly released inmates, namely the rapists, pedophiles, or anyone who has violent cases against kids."

He paused from his meal, taking a moment to process what she was saying. He took hold of his lemonade, drinking it to chase his food down. "I know you're talking about cases in the immediate area and not the entire parole list from the state? That would be more than a two-man job to go over that many files. Also, how recent are we going to check for release dates? One week or one month?" he asked, bringing things into a plausible scope of pursuing this case.

"A fifty-mile radius, anyone with rape or pedophilia on their record that was released in the last month. Then we'll narrow it down from there."

"That's good for those that registered, but not good if they're not in the system," he responded as they continued going over details to bring the case to a close. Janelle veered over to the large TV seeing the breaking news alert coming across the screen.

"Look at this," she said. He followed her eyes, tuning in to the television. They could see the cameraman zooming in on the lifeless body of a child placed in front of the elementary school. The child's face blurred out;

however, it didn't need to be seen. Each of the detectives got the same vibe, fearing this kid was connected to the to the missing child case they were called out to earlier.

"We have to go now, before the scene gets out of hand," Detective Anderson said.

"I just hope it's not the Robinson kid," Detective Tores said, not wanting to relay bad news to the mother she had promised to bring her son home safe to. Each of them having lost their appetites, they rushed out of the restaurant, jumping into their car, hitting the lights and siren, mashing the gas, and racing to the other side of the city. So many thoughts entered their minds as fast left and right turns occurred, even running red lights to get to the crime scene.

"You think it's the Robinson kid?" Detective Tores asked, fearing his response as if she was the boy's mother.

"I hope not. If it is, then we have two similar crimes within a twenty-four hour period, with one body still missing," he said, referring to Nicholas Jackson.

"How could someone want to harm a child? It's insane. We have to find out who is responsible for this, slap the cuffs on them puntas, and put them in jail forever, where they can be somebody's bitch," she let out, feeling some type of way about what was happening.

Her partner looked over at her as he drove fast to the crime scene, seeing a new side of her. Maybe this was a child kidnapping killer case. They had never taken anything like this on before, and with her being a mother, she was easily emotionally involved. It was hard not to be if you're human, he was thinking. "Janelle, I know this shit ain't right, what's going on, but I need you to have your homicide detective hat on instead of your motherly presence that will involve emotions clouding your judgment."

She took a deep breath, gazing out the window at the fast-passing cars, then back to her partner. "I'm good. My mind is in the game so we can catch this pendejo. Now I can't promise you once we get this scum, I won't put a beating on them," she responded. He gave a brief smile, thinking the same about whooping they ass, roughing them up a little.

EIGHT

Within minutes they were pulling up to the already crowded scene, no thanks to the fast-spreading social media. They parked behind the police cruisers that led the way to the taped-off area. They pushed past the crowd with their phones in hand, streaming and snapping photos. They ducked under the yellow tape, seeing Officer Jefferson.

"I hope seeing you doesn't become a routine thing in cases like this," Detective Anderson said.

"I'm not looking forward to being dispatched to scenes like this either," he responded, then added, "Anyway, our vic is a kid name Ivan Robinson between ten and twelve years old. The mother, Danika Estille, is over there losing it."

"And rightfully so," Detective Tores said, looking over at Danika on the other side of the taped-off area crying hysterically, being held back by uniformed officers. The crime scene crew was also present, working their scientific magic. They were shocked and intrigued by how clean the body was, along with how meticulously placed his body was, not randomly tossed or discarded.

Jessie Shepard was a Caucasian male standing six foot one, slim built, weighing 185 pounds. His black hair is feathered back, yet close on the side, blending with his full beard that has the natural growth going, not trimmed. Let him tell it, the ladies love it that way. This forensic special is more than a ladies' man. He's really good at this science thing, helping solve cases.

His partner is Stephanie Giacanna, an Italian American beauty with long dark brown hair she wears pulled back while working, allowing her facial features to be appreciated, coupled with her glowing light brown eyes. The five-foot-six Italian American enjoyed the challenges of the job. She viewed it as keeping her skill set sharp, making her one of the best in the city.

"Detectives, this kid is really clean. Someone went through a great deal of work to do this. You can even smell the Gain fabric softener, along with the Irish Spring soap, used to clean him up," Jessie said, pausing to point at the kid's face with his eyes still open. "He died of suffocation. The blood vessels in his eyes are ruptured."

"Is there anything that stands out to you that would give us a direction to head in?" Detective Tores asked.

"There was a note I discovered in his front left pocket," he responded, reaching into his kit where he collected the evidence. He pulled the sealed plastic bag out with the note inside, displaying it to the detectives. The note read: "I will never be bad again."

"Let me see that," JR asked, not believing someone would not only kill but also leave a note behind like this. It was a game. "This is worse than I expected. This is the beginning of this city's nightmare. Jessie, when you and Stephanie get back to the lab, let me know if you come across any little detail that will help track the person responsible for this."

"For starters, let me get that back," he said taking the note from his hands. "We will go over every inch of his body and clothing under the lights and scope to see what we come up with. Perfection doesn't exist, as much as people think. There is always something left behind, as an unwilling signature, so to speak."

"Any word on the Jackson kid yet?" Stephanie asked, knowing he was missing and there was blood at the crime scene.

"Nothing yet. I hope he's found alive so we all can be happy, mainly his mother having her child back," Detective Tores responded.

"If he's alive or dead, the person who did this may be trying to figure out what to do with him, especially now with this case placing the spotlight on child abduction. There won't be too many places to hide," Detective Anderson stated.

At the same time, Janelle looked over at Danika crying with the two officers keeping her back. She made her way over to her with hopes of consolingly the emotionally distraught mother.

"No, no, no, you promised that you would bring him home safe!" Danika yelled out, full of pain, unable to keep her tears from falling.

"I'm sorry. It's all happening so fast. I'm so sorry. We will find out who did this," Detective

Tores said before turning around, knowing there was nothing she could say or do at this very moment to change how Danika felt.

"Hey, don't let this make you lose focus. We have a job to do. That's the only promise we can make is working to the best of our abilities to track this muthafucka down," Detective Anderson said, placing his arm around his partner to cheer her up, so she could get her head back in the game.

The killer was in the midst of the crowd looking on at their work of art while the two detectives seemed to be falling apart. They enjoyed being this close, without anyone even noticing them. This alone added to the excitement and rush they were getting.

"Detectives, is this kid linked to the Jackson case last night?" a reporter yelled out. Both Janelle and JR turned to the slew of reporters and bloggers, ready to answer their questions before they started filling in the blanks on their own, creating more than what it really was.

"We're not going to exclude it from the investigation. However, we're actively working to solve both of these crimes," Detective Anderson responded.

"Is Nicholas Jackson dead or just missing, since there was blood at his crime scene?" the male reporter questioned, shocking the detectives that they knew the details of the blood.

Janelle answered this question, "As Detective Anderson mentioned, this is an ongoing investigation. There are some things we can talk about, and the other things we cannot release at this time until we catch who we're in pursuit of. In the meantime, keep your kids safe and your eyes open and cameras rolling. Who knows, you may be the one to catch this criminal in the act."

"Detectives, with one dead and one still missing, how many more cases do there need to be before we get some real answers and resolve?" the male reporter tossed out, offending both detectives.

Janelle locked eyes with the reporter, firing off her response, "I'm sorry you opted for a pussy reporter job, unlike real detective work outside of pushing paper and asking questions. We're chasing behind and tracking down real killers, with real guns and bullets. This isn't some TV show where crime gets solved by the end of the hour. This is real work that takes persistence and real skill. This is how we'll track this scum down, locking them up, giving you something worth talking about."

She didn't even give him or any other reporters a chance to toss more questions. She turned, walking away. They made it back to the car, where she continued to speak to JR, "Sorry if I came off too harshly, but he was begging for it with a question like that."

"No need to be sorry. He won't be asking dumbass questions anymore. Besides, you put everything into perspective for the reporters who think cases get solved in one hour. Good thing you didn't wait to get in the car to unleash the lady tiger on me," he said, being funny, making her laugh and bringing ease and calm back to this intense situation of trying to find this killer.

NINE

3:01 PM

As the elementary kids were being let out of school, the detectives were back at the station, looking over paper computer files of recently released rapists, pedophiles, and sexual deviants all in a fifty-mile radius.

"There are a lot of weird-looking guys I think are creepy and would never be rehabilitated. Then there are the good-looking guys you would never expect to do something so volatile," Detective Tores said, looking through the files with photos and case information beside them.

"These types of criminals that prey on the weak for sexual pleasure are the most intricate, being the ones that can deceive and mislead you. If it wasn't for DNA, a lot of these creeps, as you call them, would have never been caught."

"We have over fifty releases in the last month. The PA Parole Board is lenient toward the sexual deviants, it seems," she said, turning her face up at the thought of how these men should be in jail longer for their crimes, yet drug dealers get more time than these rapists and pedophiles. "We can first pick the ones closest to the crime and work our way out, in this fifty-mile radius."

"As long as we don't have to expand outside of the fifty-mile radius," JR responded.

"Anderson! Tores!" a loud, deep voice came through the air, from their boss, Captain Irvin Jones, a five-foot-seven, medium-built, bald-headed Afro-American with a goatee trimmed with razor perfection. His voice always commanded attention, making anyone around aware of his presence.

Each of the detectives turned to his voice.

"How are we looking with the Jackson and Robinson boys?"

"We're working hard at it, filtering through people we'll look into," Detective Tores said, then added, "Outside of that, are you having a good afternoon?"

"Not too good with this kid killed and the other still missing. We know the longer he's missing, the more likely he'll end up dead. In fact, I just got a call from Brandi Jackson, who's losing it 'cause she saw the news about the Robinson kid."

"Did you tell her we won't sleep until we get resolve?" Detective Anderson said.

"I made her aware I have my best detectives on it. So bring your A-game out to track this piece of shit down."

"This is just a thought sir," Janelle chimed in. "We can have the media outlets display recently released individuals with cases dealing with kids, to prevent them from doing it again."

"That's not good. So much blowback would come with that, from the many sensitive groups out there that protect people like that," Captain Jones said as his eyebrows turned in, thinking about how there would be good and bad. The good would be exposing these rapists and pedophiles. The bad would be the media making it known, putting a face to each of these individuals, making them targets for people who despise them.

"I'll toss that idea away, now that I think about the drama it brings. In the meantime, my partner and I will hit the pavement, coming face-to-face with these creeps we pulled off the computer in our area."

"I hope you two find your guy, so no more cases pop up, because the chief and the mayor will be breathing down my neck," he said before leaving them to do hard police work, to bring closure for the two mothers awaiting resolve.

"This child killing, along with the kidnapping, has him on edge. I hope our suspect is amongst the ones we have. Otherwise, we'll have the city in an uproar," Detective Anderson said.

"Especially if our suspect isn't done," she added, having this unsettling gut feeling that they were in for a long, dark ride. Truth be told, she wouldn't hesitate to kill this suspect if in an alleyway or house where she was the first to see or corner the suspect. For her being a mother, it would be justifiable, at the same time doing the other mothers a favor.

TEN

The killer sat in their vehicle watching the kids coming out of school, plotting their next victim. It was like being in a candy store for them, having a sweet tooth for murder. "Yes, yes, come to me, young ones. Come, allow me to welcome you to my world," the killer spoke in a low whisper, looking around as if someone could see or hear them. One of these chosen children would be coming with them today. They rolled the window down now, wanting to be seen like bait in the water, luring fish in.

A young boy was coming down the street, giving the killer butterflies, a rush even, the closer he was getting to them. They wanted this kid to pay for his sins, before taking his life, which was far from innocent. Once the kid came in earshot, the killer made their move in disguising their voice to fit with the deceptive look. “Excuse me, do you know where 1735 Zarker Street is?”

The kid stopped to answer the question, since this address was close to his house. “Yeah, it’s down a little further. You go down two more blocks, make a left at the stop sign, then a right ’cause you got to come around to go up Zarker.”

The killer acted dumbfounded, wanting to add to their lure of deception. “I’m sorry, I’m not too good with directions. I’ll give you twenty dollars to show me where it is.”

The ten-year-old was an Afro-American, medium-built boy, with innocent brown eyes and a heart and smile that were just as pure, his mother would say. He started thinking about how much junk food he could get with twenty dollars, along with buying his girl crush a snack in the cafeteria tomorrow. “Okay, I’ll do it,” he responded, getting into the car not knowing he had just sealed his own fate.

“Here’s your twenty bucks, Michael,” the killer said in a low, sadistic whisper that instantly made Michael alert. He even was caught off guard at how this complete stranger knew his name. As he processed all of this in the seconds upon closing the car door, he reached back for the door handle to flee, to no avail.

He felt a pinching in his neck as the killer poked him with a needle, sending a sedative surging through his body. "What you do that for?" Michael asked before going unconscious with his hand on the door handle.

The killer reacting fast, not wanting to be compromised, took hold of Michael, securing the door, before putting the car in drive, getting a rush, driving off, looking at themselves in the rearview mirror, and coming to the Stop sign. "Should I make a left or right, Michael? I forgot what you said," the killer taunted, amusing themselves. The disguise the killer wore had come from a well-known website for costumes and makeup. Even the Hollywood actors used it, transforming themselves into any race, younger, older, male or female characters. So if anyone did happen to capture this abduction trying to describe them, it would be of no use. Even the car they were in was stolen, and when they were done, it would be wiped downed and maybe burned to alleviate any traces of their presence.

"Today is going to be a good day, Michael. We're going to have so much fun," the killer taunted, driving until they saw blue and red flashing lights coming fast behind them as they were driving down Market Street. The killer tensed up, looking over at Michael, who was out cold leaning against the door. How could they explain their way out of this? Should I keep going? So many thoughts entered the killer's mind, fearing capture, especially knowing what they did to people like this in prison, if the cops didn't kill them first.

"I guess this is the end. No fun for us, Michael," the killer said, pulling over. At the same time, the cop car zoomed past, speeding up to the crime scene he had gotten the call to. The killer let out a heavy sigh and started laughing in a tormented, sadistic way. "That was close, Michael. Now let's get to it before they ruin what I have in store for you," they said, driving off, feeling victorious over this moment of being back in control to kidnap and murder.

ELEVEN

Detectives Tores and Anderson selected four names from the bunch they had. These four recently released offenders would be the ones they looked into today. The first on the list was a parolee that lived in the Hallmanor projects, also known as the South Acres. It was a place most cops preferred to drive through, not walk on foot, because of the level of violence, even cop shootings. There were so many outs for people to run through, and some places were dead ends, which is even more deadly to be caught in if you're not from or welcomed to this project. The detectives were accompanied by one uniformed officer in his squad car.

"48 I, that's the place right there," Detective Tores said, pointing at the numbered row homes.

"You ready to do this without losing control, so we can get answers?"

"I'm good over here. Now let's get to it. We have a lot of work to do," she responded, stepping out of the car, securing her sidearm and unbuttoning the holster.

The drug lookouts whistled as they exited the car, getting the attention of everyone moving around illegally. "We're homicide. We come when you kill over your drugs," Detective Tores said, making JR laugh as they headed to the address on the paper where Pete Richardson lived. She knocked on the door, and moments later, a young female came to the door pregnant, looking barely legal.

"Can I help y'all?" she asked, rubbing her belly that was full and round, visibly close to her due date.

"Is Pete Richardson here?" Tores asked.

"Nah, he just went down to the chinks corner store to get some snacks I was craving."

"What is your relation to Mr. Richardson? You look a bit young to be his girlfriend," Detective Tores questioned. The young girl rolled her eyes and smacked her teeth, feeling disrespected. The look she was giving Janelle was piercing as she responded, displaying how offended she was.

"First off, Mrs. Thing, he's my big brother. Second, for your information, I will be a good mother, no matter how old I am, so don't judge me."

As Janelle was going back and forth with the young female, Detective Anderson noticed Pete coming from the Chinese store, just as his sister said. "Tores, here comes our guy now," he said, nodding his head in Pete's direction. JR gestured for Pete to hurry up, so they could get the questions and answers out of the way, so they could go to the next person of interest's house.

Suddenly, Pete stopped looking at the uniformed officer along with the two detectives standing in front of his house. He remembered the two detectives' faces from the news. "Why are they here?" he was thinking, hoping they were not trying to play him. Instinctively, the flight and fear kicked in. Thinking about jail, he turned quickly and took off running toward the other projects connected to Hallmanor—Hoover Holmes on 13th Street.

Seeing him abruptly take off gave both detectives a surge of adrenaline, making them feel as if he was their guy. JR passed the folder to the uniformed officer before taking off running behind him. JR was fast, always running on the days he wasn't going to the gym. Janelle was also in shape, not far behind JR, who was taking long, fast strides, thrusting his feet into the pavement, pushing him forward faster and faster, at the same time sucking in gulps of warm air, fueling the chase.

"What are you running for, Pete?" Detective Anderson yelled out. Could he be our killer? Does he have information on who the killer is? These are all questions he now wants to know, with him running away. Pete glanced over his shoulder, seeing the fast-approaching detectives closing in on him. In the split seconds it took for him to look back as he was running across Thirteenth Street, a car came fast, slamming into his frame, thrusting his body close to thirty feet away, before he came down hard on the ground.

"Oh shit," Detective Anderson expressed shock by the violent accident. The Lexus 600

Hybrid that slammed into him came to a screeching halt. “Let me see your hands!” Detective Anderson said.

Detective Anderson closed in on Pete with his gun aimed at him, in case he tried to flee or shoot his way out of capture. “You could have avoided all of this. We only wanted to ask you a few questions,” Detective Anderson said, breathing heavy, backed by his adrenaline being spiked by the chase. Pete has now suffered a broken leg and arm and a few ribs, which have punctured his lung, which is clear to the detectives, seeing the bubbles of blood spewing from his mouth, trying to speak. The blood is replacing the oxygen he needs to make it through this painful situation he foolishly placed himself in.

“I, I, I did—didn’t want to go, go to jail,” Pete managed to get out before he started grunting from the intense pain his body was experiencing at this moment. He started choking and coughing as the blood filled up his lungs. Detective Tores immediately made the call for medical attention, as did the locals seeing the accident.

"You're going to be okay, Pete. Help is coming," Detective Tores said, then added, "Help us find Nicholas Jackson, if you know who kidnapped him. Tell us who killed the Robinson kid," she asked, staring at him, seeing his eyes widening as if he wanted to say something. The truth maybe? A painful smirk graced his face briefly as death was fast approaching.

"It, it, was—wasn't me," Pete said before blood forced its way out of his mouth and nose, suffocating him, his eyes widened in fear as death came snatching his soul from his flesh, taking him on a dark journey. His body ceased all movement.

"Don't fucking die yet, punta. Tell me more," Detective Tores said, feeling like he had the answers they were looking for.

"Detective Tores, that's enough. You're not going to get anything from a dead man. Plus, we have cameras out here," he said, referring to everybody in the projects with their cell phones out, along with the driver of the Lexus filming the body and their car, for insurance reasons.

"What the fuck y'all do to my brother!" the dead man's sister came up screaming aggressively, holding her pregnant belly. When she came around and saw her brother's eyes open, with no life in them, she snapped. "Y'all think shit is sweet around here? You can't come into this hood killing us and get away with it!" Pete's sister Trina shouted aggressively, getting the attention of the thugs in the hood so they could stand with her. At the same time she removed a chrome .32 automatic, one in the chamber, safety off, and fired on Detective Anderson back to back, sending slugs crashing into his chest, pushing him back and making him lose balance and fall to the ground. At the same time Trina shifted her pistol to Detective Tores, who she also had the drop on. Suddenly, gunfire came from the uniformed officer, gunning the pregnant Trina down with multiple .45 automatic slugs. While her body was falling, gunfire from the crowd erupted. Slugs came targeting the police officer that shot Trina along with the detectives.

"Shots fired! Officer down!" Detective Tores yelled through the radio, giving her location to the dispatcher. All officers and detectives in the area of the city came fast, knowing this was a high-crime and dangerous area. Janelle dropped down to JR's side. "JR, you okay?" she asked, shaken with all that had taken place so fast.

Detective Anderson took a deep breath, thanking God for the bulletproof vest that stopped the .32 caliber slugs. "I'll be fine. That shit knocked the wind out of me, but I'm good. She was trippin'." He responded, rubbing his hand over his chest where the slugs crashed into the vest. Janelle helped him to his feet, over to one of the ambulances that had just pulled up. Detective Anderson wasn't too worried about himself; he would live. He wanted the medics to focus on the uniformed officer that was bleeding since he caught slugs in the arm and legs. JR and Janelle left, heading to the next person of interest, hoping it went better than this intense situation.

TWELVE

The first five minutes of the ride to the next suspect's house, the car was silent as each of them took in the magnitude of what had just taken place. Neither of them expected what happened to unfold as it did. "God's on your side. He knows we have a case to close and that I wouldn't be able to find another partner as good as you," she said, breaking the silence.

"Or as good looking, since you're on a roll," he responded, being funny.

"Don't push it, JR. You know the rules of being my partner. Look, don't touch, because it wouldn't be good if it didn't work, or we crossed that line and remained partners."

"I get it, you want me to quit in order to have a chance with you," he said, then added, "I wouldn't get tired of seeing you all day every day."

She smiled, reaching down and turning the radio on. "Whatever you do at this next house, don't chase anyone."

"He was guilty of something; otherwise, he wouldn't have taken off like that. Call it karma," he responded. "Lewis Lexiton is our next guy," he added.

Lewis, age thirty, was a big fella, standing five foot eleven and weighing close to three hundred pounds. He was Afro-American, with dark skin, and from the looks of his photo, he had a thick black beard and afro cut that he could easily braid if he chose.

"It don't look like he worked out a day upstate in the yard."

"He probably was fantasizing about his niece and nephew he assaulted."

"Good thing is, he won't be doing any running unless food is involved," JR said, getting a laugh from his partner. Lewis lived on 19th and Market Streets, the corner house. He'd been living there since his release. They exited the car, walked up the steps, and knocked on the door, followed by ringing the doorbell. Both detectives had information on the previous crime he did time for. Now they had to see what he knew, if anything at all, about the case they had open.

"Do you think Pete had a partner in crime?" Detective Tores asked.

"No. These types of criminals work alone, so they can isolate their victims."

Bringing their conversation to a halt, the front door opened up. There stood Lewis Lexiton in the flesh, his eyes wide with surprise, almost like he was up to something.

"Lewis, this is Detective Tores. I'm Detective Anderson. We're with Homicide. We would like to ask you a few questions."

Lewis was breathing abnormally like he was upstairs rushing down to answer the door.

"Why are you breathing so heavily? Were you working out?" Detective Tores asked, knowing he wasn't working anything out if it wasn't at the dinner table.

"I, I was working on something in the basement when I heard the doorbell ring. Look at me; I'm not in the best shape," he responded.

"Can we come in?" she asked, becoming serious.

He welcomed them in, not wanting to be confrontational. "Yeah, what y'all want to ask me?"

"About the Robinson and Jackson kids," Detective Anderson said.

"I saw those kids on the news," he responded, sitting across from them on the sofa, remaining calm as if he knew they were coming to harass him. He sat with his arms crossed, ready to see what they had to say.

"Lewis we have had a tense day thus far, so we'll be up front with our questions just as we expect with your answers."

"No problem, lady."

"It's Detective Tores," she expressed.

"Where were you last night between nine and ten?" JR asked.

"Here watching CSI Las Vegas."

"You watch to learn how to cover your tracks?" Detective Tores asked sarcastically.

"It's entertainment yet educating. The reality is, no one solves crimes in one hour," he shot back with her words to the reporter. Her face balled up, not liking it how he tossed her words back so smoothly.

"Is there anyone who can vouch for your whereabouts?" JR asked. "Yes, I'm on house arrest."

"That doesn't mean anything. You can sneak out when you want," Detective Tores said.

Lewis raised his leg, pulling his pant leg up, displaying the ankle monitor. "These things work well. At exactly 9:00 PM it's activated by that machine right there."

Both detectives felt like they hit a brick wall with Lewis, yet they were still not going to let him off so easily. "What time does it turn off?" Detective Tores asked.

"6:00 AM."

"Tell us your whereabouts starting at six until now," she wanted to know, seeing if there was any discrepancy.

He squirmed in his seat, adjusting himself, seeming uncomfortable. Then a smirk graced his face that both detectives picked up on. "I got up for work and had to be in by seven. I was there until three. Rushed from work to the parole office. I left there five minutes to four. I got home twenty after four, showered, and ate. Now I'm here with you two. Now if you want the recipe or ingredients to my dinner, I got that too," he added, being smart.

As those words flowed from his mouth, an abrupt thump sound came from the basement, alerting the detectives. "What the fuck was that?" Detective Anderson asked.

Lewis froze in thought, and then it came to him. "Oh shit, my forty ounce of Old English I had sitting on the washer 'cause I was doing laundry. It must be on spin cycle shaking my beer off. I guess I have a mess to clean up," he responded with a grin on his face.

Detective Anderson was getting a strange vibe about this Lewis guy. "What is it?" he wondered, looking on at this fat muthafucka looking so calm, like he was in control. It had been a long day thus far. He and his partner were in need of caffeine and food to fuel their bodies and keep their minds sharp.

"We're done here, partner. Lewis, don't get too comfortable, fat boy. We'll be back if something comes up pointing back at you."

Detective Anderson said, giving Lewis a dark stare trying to cut through his calm demeanor, seeing what secrets and kids he kept.

"Aye, ma, I don't want no problems. I'm staying out of trouble and out of the way," Lewis said, walking the detectives to the door. In his mind, he was thinking: Now get the fuck out of my house, so I can finish taking care of business. As soon as they exited, he went back down to the basement.

THIRTEEN

When the detectives came out of the house, they noticed young teens sitting on their car. "Get you badasses of my car, before I lock all you little muthafuckas up!" Detective Anderson said, rushing over to the kids, who took off running, looking back at him. He didn't chase after them. He only wanted them off the car. "What the hell is wrong with these kids?"

"They knew this is our car. They wanted to look tough or prove themselves by bouncing on it and chilling like they run these streets."

"They need to be at home with their parents, especially with these recent cases jumping off. I know if I had kids, they would be at home right now," he said, getting into the car at the same time his cell phone was sounding off. He noticed the incoming call was Jessie with the crime scene crew. "Tell me something good, Jessie, so I can sleep good tonight."

"The Robinson kid suffered multiple blows to the head, leaving a hematoma, but the cause of death is indeed suffocation."

"Get to the real shit that will help me hammer this muthafucka."

"Transfer, I found a synthetic strand of grayish-colored hair. It's the same type of material found in wigs or weaves, depending on the quality. It could also come from a toupee."

"So we're looking for someone bald or old?"

"I present the evidence. It's up to you guys to find what direction you want to go after that."

"If you find anything else that would give us more direction, get back to us," he said, ending the call, checking the time and seeing they'd been going at it all day. "It's time to wrap this day up, as much as we want to be out here all day and night. You have a son that needs you."

"That's sweet of you to think of my son. I will give him a big hug and kiss from you, for your thoughtfulness." He laughed at her, knowing she was joking about it. They made it back to the station to turn the car in and punch out, when they saw Captain Jones in the parking garage.

"Anderson! Tores! I hope you two are making some progress with this case. Oh, and what the hell happened out at the south side projects today? You better be thanking God for the vest. No more distractions like that. We need to focus on this kidnapping and child killing."

"Everything is under control sir. That shit out there shouldn't have gone down like that. You know they're really wild out the South Acres. Outside of that, we're pursuing the leads we have," Detective Anderson said.

Captain Jones didn't respond. He just got into his car, ending the conversation, something he was known to do once he had spoken his mind.

"Okay, I guess he's done talking to us?" Detective Tores said, then added, "Have a good night, JR. I'll see you first thing in the morning. Oh, I'm also thankful for the vest you wore today." She tapped him on the shoulder before getting out and going to her car. He did the same, driving home with so many thoughts about how's this case was going to come to an end. He didn't care too much for these types of people preying on children, so there's going to be many late nights of thinking of how to track this scum down, making them pay in full.

FOURTEEN

The killer was heading down to the cold basement after being distracted. The ten-year-old Michael Miller was now bound at the ankles, his hands secured above his head, tied to the beam running across the basement ceiling. His eyes were covered, leaving him in the darkness. His screams and pleas were muffled by the gag in his mouth. This feeling of being mute wasn't sitting well with him. In fact, the fear he was feeling because of it was making him struggle to be released. He really hated that he was stripped of all his clothing, making him not only feel the cold floor beneath him, but also violated and vulnerable. The killer came up behind Michael, wrapping their arms around him. Their cold hands felt like the floor, sending chills and fear racing through his body, making him squirm, all to no use.

"You should be so lucky, Michael. I selected you, making you the chosen one, except you don't have any powers or abilities. The power is mine, all mine," the killer whispered close up against Michael's ear, taunting him as he shook, trembling with fear. They released the arm from around his neck, stepping back, turning the music on, sounds of a violin setting the mood as they turned back around with a hammer in hand.

"Let's play doctor. I'm going to test your reflexes," they said, pretending to play the hammer like a violin, their eyes closed as if waiting for the right moment. Then it happened. Their eyes opened, the simulation of playing the violin halted, and they swung the hammer with force into the side of Michael's head, slamming into his temple. Michael's screams and attempts to be set free stopped as his body went limp, from being brutally knocked unconscious. His temple immediately swelled, looking like a kiwi-sized knot pulsating, looking like it was ready to burst. Michael's body hung from his wrist, being tied to the beam. The killer, still in tune with the rhythm of the violin playing on the radio, waltzed around to the other side of Michael.

"Now, now, no sleeping. That's not a good reflex," they said, swinging the hammer hard, crashing into his other side in the temple. Michael's body started shaking, convulsing violently, having a seizure.

"Oooh, what do we have here?" the killer questioned, standing back and watching his body shaking, reacting to the violent trauma imposed on it. His body released urine and feces the more he shook, and grunting sounds could be heard, almost like he was fighting through the pain. Instead, the darkness of death came over his young flesh as he came to a halt, expelling a grunting breath as life escaped his young flesh.

"Are you done, Michael? Don't be a quitter," the killer said, coming to the front of him, checking his breathing and pulse. He was gone, dead to the world. "Now I have to find someone else to play with," the killer said, placing the hammer on the table before taking the blindfold and gag off of Michael. The killer leaned in, smelling his flesh that had death creeping over it. The rush of murder raced through their body as they inhaled and exhaled. For the killer, it was only about murder, making them pay for their sins.

One would think child kidnapping and killing is about being a sexual deviant. Not for this person. Like most hunters, it was about the kill. The killer, being a perfectionist that was out of touch with reality, took the body down and cleaned it up, along with all of his clothing. Once they had him ready, they took him to the location he would be discovered, noticing the cards, balloons, and candles in memory of Ivan Robinson.

"What do we have here, Michael? Since you're joining the party, they'll give you balloons and cards too," the killer said, slipping away undetected, leaving his body to be discovered by those paying respects to the Robinson kid.

FIFTEEN

Janelle stepped out of the shower, which had allowed her mind and body to be at ease after a long day's work. She stood looking in the mirror, thinking about catching this monster that had stunned the city with their antics. Being a mother, it was hard for her not to take it hard or personally. For her, family was everything, so she felt for the mothers.

When she exited the bathroom, her mother, Margarita, called out to her, "Janelle, mi hija, yo tengo comer para ti," she said, allowing her to know she had food for her.

"Espera in minute, mami. I just got out of the shower."

Margarita was a short, heavy-set Latina with curly black hair. She loved her makeup that made her look younger, or so she always said. The mother of one spoiled her only grandson and daughter, staying home babysitting and cooking food for her daughter after long days of work. She also knew that Janelle would skip meals with her focus on cases sometimes, so she had to make sure she stayed on top of her with that. Margarita was also worried, having seen the news with the child-killing and kidnapping, plus the shoot-out earlier today, out the south side projects.

Janelle came downstairs in her Puerto Rican-flag-print pajamas. She hugged her son, giving him motherly kisses, making him laugh. “I miss you, mi hijo,” she said, kissing his cheek once more, appreciating this moment with her son, knowing there are mothers out there who wouldn’t have this chance again.”

“Mi hija, asiento esta ahora comer. I made some comfort food you like. Pork chops, yellow rice with black beans, green peppers, onions, with a bean gravy on the side,” Margarita said, looking on at her daughter.

“Gracias, mi amor. I really do appreciate you and all you do, Mama.”

“I know, mi hija.” She went into the kitchen and prepared a plate before coming back and placing the food down in front of her. Then she took hold of her grandson, Pito, so she could eat. She sat at the other end of the table, looking back at her daughter.

"Mi hija, I saw you on television today, looking a little unprofessional. You can't let this case get to you. Por amor de Dios, I need you to be safe out there. I also saw that shooting, es no bueno."

"It's going to be all right, ma. As for that punta that did that to the Robinson boy, we'll get them," she said, taking a bite of her pork chop.

"You know you could have been a lawyer or a doctor, saving people's lives, not this dangerous cop stuff, chasing behind people that don't want to go to jail. You see what happened to your partner. I would lose my mind, mi hija, if someone did that to you. Yeah, it was all over Twitter, and that Instagram thing. These kids record everything, like it's a game. For me, it's no game when it comes to my child," Margarita said, being an old school Latina from Ponce, Puerto Rico. She would snap tracking down the person who brought harm to her daughter. Being raised in the hood, having to pull the trigger for dope boys back home, she was no stranger to violence. She just didn't want to be a part of it anymore. That's why she moved to the United States when she was twenty-one.

Janelle didn't want her mom worrying about her, especially hearing the tone in her voice. "Everything is going to be fine, Ma. I promise. God is also watching over me, because he wanted me to be a cop, to track down all the bad guys," Janelle said with a smile and partially full mouth.

"Okay, mi hija, buenos noches. I'm going to bed to get some rest. I need it to keep up with you and my grandson," Margarita said, getting up from the table.

"Good night, Mama. I love you, and don't worry about me too much. I'm a big girl, a cop with a gun," Janelle said, being funny.

"I'm your mother. It's my job to worry. When Pito grows up, you'll understand," she responded, heading up the steps, leaving her to think of her words while enjoying the food cooked with a mother's love.

SIXTEEN

7:16 AM

The next day, Janelle was awakened by her mother's voice calling out to her. "Janelle, adonde tu hijo?" she asked where Pito was. When Janelle opened her eyes, she saw he wasn't snuggled up behind her legs as he was when she fell asleep downstairs on the couch. She jumped up in fear, thinking the worst with all that had been taking place.

"Ma, he wasn't upstairs with you?" Her voice displayed fear.

"I came down here to wake you up for work, since I heard your alarm clock going off."

"No, no. Pito! Pito!" Janelle called out, running up the stairs to his bedroom. She rushed inside his room. He was not in sight. Her heart dropped, fearing he was missing. She turned around, running into her bedroom. He was not on the bed. She came over to turn the loud alarm clock off, only to see her son on the side of the bed trying to turn the alarm clock off. This allowed a sense of calm and relief to come to her as she dropped down to her knees by her son.

"Clock too loud, Mama. It wake me up," Pito said, since he came up to her room to fall back to sleep, thinking she would find her way up to the room too.

She turned the alarm off for him before giving him a big hug and kiss. "I love you, baby."

"I love you too, Mama," he responded. Margarita came into the room caressing Janelle's back, seeing how distressed she was. She also knew this was God's way of showing Janelle how her mother also worries. She didn't verbalize it; however, Janelle felt and knew it.

Her cell phone sounded off, shifting her attention. She stood looking at her phone on the nightstand. It was JR. She picked up on the third ring. "Good morning, partner, tell me the bad news," she said knowing he didn't call this early for nothing.

"We have another child victim. I'll fill you in on details when I get to your place. We'll head to the crime scene from there."

"I'll be ready when you get here," she said, ending the call, hugging her son once more before saying, "Mommy's got to go get the bad guys, baby, okay?"

"Yeah, get all the bad guys," Pito said, looking up at his mother.

"Ma, I love you, and I am thankful for everything you do," Janelle said, giving her mom a hug before rushing to get herself together. It didn't take long before she secured her vest, side arm, and .25 automatic she put on the ankle holster. She had this bad gut feeling about the day ahead, especially how it started from the moment she woke up. She headed downstairs, preparing to leave, having heard the horn honking a few times on the way down the steps.

"Ma, I'm about to leave. I'll see you and Pito later."

"Be careful, mi hija ."

"I will, Ma," she said, walking out the door, over to the car.

Her partner looked like he had tossed and turned all night. He flipped the lights and sirens on soon as she got it in, at the same time mashing the gas. "So far, the victim is unidentified."

"What? What type of parents does this kid have, not reporting him missing? So it's not the Jackson kid?"

"I don't think so. The officer would have noticed him from the photos."

"I bet your fat friend Lewis Lexiton did this shit. We should have checked his basement when we heard that noise. The kid could have been struggling to break free," Detective Tores said, thinking back to that moment, hearing the sound.

"It was glass breaking. He said it was his forty-ounce beer, falling off the washer."

"How convenient, and we brought that line. It's what he wanted us to believe. It could've been someone trying to escape."

"Now you make me want to bust his fat ass and get a warrant to search his house."

"We don't need a warrant with probable cause. We have a child-murdering case, and we heard noise, plus he's a person of interest. We do what we want, most of all what needs to be done to keep these streets and kids safe," she said firmly. It also made him look at her in a different light, seeing this aggressive side of her that mirrored the way he handled things. "From now on, no loose ends," he said, becoming even more focused.

SEVENTEEN

It didn't take long before they were pulling up to the elementary school, where the body was laid out, just like the previous murder victim. The crime scene crew, Stephanie and Jessie, were also present, along with a crowd of people standing recording with their phones, always too late, never capturing this killer on video.

"Good morning, Detectives, it's like déjà vu all over again. One of the teachers found this kid. She identified him as Michael Miller of Zarker Street. The mother is Nikia Miller. She's being brought out here now. The officers said she's wreaking of alcohol, so it explains why she didn't notice he was missing and didn't come home last night," Officer Jefferson said.

"Appreciate the update. This isn't good, meeting like this, as I stated before, especially with you being the first officer on the scene. Let's hope this cycle doesn't continue to repeat itself," Detective Anderson stated. Then he made his way over to Jessie and Stephanie.

"Is it the same MO?" Detective Tores asked.

"So far, it looks like it, with the body being staged here. As for the visual assessment, blunt force trauma," Stephanie responded while continuing to process the area and body. Jessie removed two plastic bags from his kit, standing to his feet, showing the detectives that another note was discovered.

Detective Anderson snatched it from Jessie's hand to read it. "I will never do what I did again." His eye rose, angling in, trying to figure out what it meant and why is this sadistic son of a bitch was leaving notes behind.

"The muthafucka is trippin' with these stupid ass notes, like this is a game or something. I should leave a note right here letting this killer know that when we track them, they might not be so lucky to have the comfort of a jail cell," Detective Anderson snapped.

"We found more grayish hairs on the boy's clothing. Outside of that, the body was cleaned. We will comb the body and clothing for more once we get back to the lab." Jessie stated.

Detective Tores stood to the side looking down at the lifeless body of this young kid, wondering to herself what this kid could have possibly done wrong to deserve this type of treatment and end to his young life. This was truly a mother's worst fear, losing a child. It imposed the feeling of helplessness while ripping out her heart, being tormented by the emotions that come with it.

"Stephanie, did you or Jessie have time to pull prints off the previous note?" Detective Tores questioned.

"Nothing. This killer is meticulous when it comes to detail. The only thing is the synthetic fibers of the grayish hairs."

"When a person is this detailed, for them to leave the hair behind could easily be misdirection," Stephanie pointed out.

"We need to shut down all directions, to close in on this piece of shit," Detective Tores stated. None of them realized the killer was standing close by hearing their words, now knowing what they felt and thought, though far enough away from them not to be noticed, standing behind the yellow tape.

"We should have a unit sit on the school or away from this area to catch or deter them. If one of the students would have discovered these bodies, they would have a lifetime of mental and emotional trauma," Detective Tores said.

"It's evident this crazy muthafucka has some type of attachment to this school, for them to leave the kids here," Detective Anderson said, then added, when he heard the screaming female pushing through the crowd, accompanied by officers, "Here comes the drama and tears."

"Noooo! Not my baby boy! Move out of my way! Let me see my baby!" she yelled out, closing in on the yellow tape slipping under it. "Why? Why did this happen to my baby?" she cried out, dropping to her knees, unable to take any more steps toward his lifeless body, knowing it was him and he was no more. The twenty-seven-year-old drunken mother fainted in pain, regretting her alcoholic choices that allowed this to even take place.

The detectives, along with the crime scene crew, could smell the alcohol permeating from her body as they helped her to her feet, bringing her back around. The officers took her to get medical attention and the rehab that was much needed to cope with all she was experiencing. The detectives noticed Brandi Jackson speaking to the media and bloggers, crying, wiping her tears, fearing her son may also end up like this, since he hadn't been found.

"We should go see what that's all about," Detective Tores said.

"Okay. We don't want her thinking we ain't working on her case, to prevent this shit from happening to her son." As soon as they approached, the cameras shifted toward them, zooming in.

"Detectives! Detectives! Ms. Jackson fears her son will end up like this. Can you reassure her this won't happen to her son?"

"With all these cases taking place so fast, we're gathering evidence just as fast with hopes of closing in on this suspected child killer. We can assure this city and Ms. Jackson that we're going to do all it takes to bring this person down," Detective Anderson stated.

"Detective, can you elaborate on this evidence you mentioned?"

"We're trying to catch this killer, not let them know what we know," he responded.

"What significance does leaving these kids' bodies here have?"

"I got this, partner," Janelle said, taking lead on the question. "The killer may have gone to this school, where they faced bullying or other haunting memories. They can also be employed here. We're not going exclude any plausible scenarios or suspects. As my partner stated, we will use all resources to close this case, sooner than later. In the meantime, all schools will be monitored. We suggest the parents out there keep their children close, having their children never walk alone, in groups if they can."

"So you're asking the community to assist you two in doing your job?" Tom Taylor, the reporter, said. "This is a homicide case that is extremely of serious nature.

"You may not be from the city, so tipping cows may be the big event where you live. This is murder. It takes a village to raise a kid, just as it takes our city to make sure we protect them," Detective Tores said firmly, not allowing herself to be as she was yesterday. The killer slipped away into the crowd when the detectives got closer, speaking to the media. They didn't want to wear out their welcome. They already got what they came for, which was a rush out of seeing the lifeless body once more before they took him away. Also, being this close to the detectives and watching them work added to their level of excitement.

EIGHTEEN

"I have an unsettling vibe about this case, kind of like it's going to get worse before it gets better," Detective Anderson said, driving off. "What gets me so far is the Jackson kid is still missing, which means he may not be connected to this car, and we now have to focus solely on a child killer while hoping the Missing Persons division follows through on the case," Detective Tores stated.

JR's cell phone started ringing. He checked the incoming call and saw it was Captain Jones. "It's your favorite person, Janelle. You want to answer it?" he asked. At the same time she looked to see who the caller was.

"You're a big boy. You can handle it," she responded, knowing the captain's voice could leap through the phone at times, especially when he was upset, and that was pretty much always, working this job.

He accepted the call, placing it on speaker. "Anderson here."

"What the hell is going on out there? This is not how I wanted to start my day! I just got a call from the chief, who was at home watching it on the news. And the Jackson kid's mother was crying and pleading for closure in having her son back. I need you and Tores in my office before the day is over with." He hung up before they could even respond.

"He's going to give himself a heart attack with all that yelling he does," Janelle said.

"In the meantime, we have to get some resolve, to prevent being so many steps behind this scum. For starters, we're going to pay fat-ass Lewis Lexiton a visit, then the other names on our list," JR said, driving to his house. Once they pulled up on the house, they exited, rushing up on the steps, ready to stir him up, to see what he was hiding, if anything at all. They knocked on the door a few times, followed by the doorbell. Minutes passed by with no answer. "I just remembered he did say he worked between these hours when he explained his day to us yesterday," Detective Tores said. As those words flowed from her mouth, Lewis popped into the living room window, looking out.

"Look at this muthafucka right here. He took a day off from work, huh?" Detective Anderson said, staring at Lewis who was looking startled to see them again. "Open the door. We need to holla at you about that noise we heard in your basement yesterday."

"What? Y'all trippin'. I ain't letting you in without a warrant," he responded, making the detectives think he had even more of a reason to hide something. Whatever it was, he didn't want them to know about it. For all they knew, it could be another kid, the next victim even? They couldn't risk walking away again, having another kid show up dead somewhere. They would never forgive themselves.

"If you want to talk to me, call my lawyer, Brian Walk." A surging rage came over the two of them, forcing them to remove their side arms, ready to kick the front door in.

"Tores you know like I know, we don't have time for lawyers and warrants. We leave, it gives him more time to clear the house and maybe vanish." Each of them also knew that without a warrant, whatever they discovered would never stand up in court. For them, if they could save a child, that'd be justice enough. The rest would follow.

Lewis, seeing the looks on their faces, knew they were about to do something, so he moved quickly, disappearing from the window. His sudden movement only alerted them even more, making Detective Anderson thrust his foot into the front door with brute force, making it swing open. They rushed in, guns out at the ready, fingers inside their trigger guards up against the trigger, ready to down this fat son of a bitch.

Detective Tores came up quickly, placing her pistol to his head, stopping him at the top of the basement step. "I swear, you move, and your brains will beat your body down the steps, punta!" she said.

"What you hiding down there, fat boy? It better not be a kid, because I promise you, if it is, we'll drive you far from here to a corn field in Amish country and leave you full of bullet holes," Detective Anderson said, staring at Lewis.

"It's, it's not what you think, man. I'm not a fucking child molester or killer. I never was. My sisters set me so they could take my money," he said nervously, in fear of what they were about to discover.

"Money, huh?" Tores said in disbelief.

At the same JR checked out the brand-new clothing he had on plus the Gucci store bags by the couch. "So you're telling me and my partner the charges you had were bogus and this big-time lawyer you have didn't get you out of it?"

"Bruh, I ain't lying. The niggas from my hood know how real I am. That's why I didn't have no beef upstate."

"You're hiding something, fat boy, so lead the way down the steps," Tores said, nudging her gun to the back of his head. His body tensed up, feeling the gun to his head, knowing the safety was off and she could easily blow his brains out, then walked away as if they were never there. As soon as they came downstairs to the basement, they noticed the bricks of cocaine still wrapped in black plastic, along with a pile of cocaine and a digital scale with large plastic bags for distribution. There were at least five or six kilos plus the brick of power he had open. What really caught their attention was the bag of money on the floor by the table of cocaine.

"How many bricks you got right there?" JR asked.

"Six plus the one I'm breaking down."

"You a real hood boss on the low, huh? What them bricks going for, forty-five bands these days with the drought?"

Lewis's eyebrows shifted, shocked that a homicide cop would know so much about the drug trade. "It's over three hundred stacks in work, but you know I'll beat this shit in court. It wouldn't make it past the preliminary," Lewis said, knowing his legal rights. Detective Anderson also knew this. He even knew Lewis wasn't the guy he was chasing after either, but he couldn't walk away leaving this amount of drugs to hit the streets either.

"Today's your lucky day. Take the unlawful bid you did as payment for the drugs you have here. Charge this loss to the game," Detective Anderson said. He also took the stacks of money that were on the table too. It was close to a quarter million.

"Why you taking my money, bruh? I need that to get back."

"You should be thanking me. As for this paper, consider it bail money, 'cause you're a free man when we walk out of here," Detective Anderson said, placing the money and drugs in the bag before rolling out.

"Y'all some greedy muthafuckas taking my money. You think my connect is going let that fly?" he said, speaking about the Dominicans he got his product from.

JR ignored him, getting into the car and driving off. A few minutes later, Janelle spoke on what had just taken place. "I'm all for moving out when I thought he was a kid creep, but taking the money?"

"We did the city and drug task force a favor today taking the coke off the streets. Now the money, we can split it if you want, or we can put it up as the reward to help track this child killer and kidnapper out there."

"I thought you were going rogue on me," she said, looking on at him.

"I'm the good cop, always remember that. I may have some fucked-up tactics to get crimes solved, but at the end of the day, I'm here to protect my city. Now the money, we put it to good use. If we catch the killer first, then it still will be put to good use, on a much-needed vacation," he said being real and funny at the same time.

"Now I could go for a trip to Puerto Rico, papi," she said, smiling, thinking about a nice vacation with her mom and son in their home country. JR pulled up to the large green dumpster, where he disposed of the bag with the bricks of cocaine in it. It would later find its way to the land fields, burning with the rest of the trash. Seeing him do this also placed Janelle at ease, knowing the drugs wouldn't affect families or children in this city.

NINETEEN

The killer was back at it again, this time, having the media and community involved. In fact, they were a part of the community, they were thinking, as they drive down Rudy Road, noticing their next potential victim walking to school, which was four blocks away. His mother didn't bother walking with him, even amidst all that had been taken place. She was too busy on the phone gossiping with her friend.

The killer, being a trusted member of the community, no one would ever suspect them, especially having this disguise on. They drove slowly, alongside the walking kid, getting a rush out of this moment, like a hunter closing in on their kill. They started looking in all directions as their blood pumped, preparing to close in on this kid. Nothing, no one in sight. "This feels so good," they were thinking. Those that were out, were too concerned with their own children. No one was looking. "This is almost like a fat kid at a buffet for the first time, seeing so many selections of food down to the perfect cut of steak, so juicy and just right for the taking," the psycho killer said in this taunting, low whisper, zooming in on the young boy waking alone. The young boy now noticed the van driving alongside of him at the same pace, so he looked toward the van to see if he noticed the driver. He didn't recognize them.

"What the fuck you looking at?" the young boy said to the driver, who seemed to turn away, looking forward, yet still keeping pace with the young boy, who was picking up his pace, walking faster.

"Oh, you're going to play hard to get, huh?" the killer said, bringing the van to a sudden halt as the driver's door opened at the same time.

The young boy noticed this. His heart started beating fast, just as his young mind started racing, thinking about the other two boys killed along with the one missing. He was now two and a half blocks away from the school and closing, walking faster, toting his Lakers book bag with his lunch and homework.

He looked back at the van and saw the driver of the van exit, looking like they were preparing to run after him. He wasn't about to let that happen, so his fast pace picked up to a jog.

"You trippin', you ain't going get me," the young boy said, being in shape from the sports activities he loved playing in and out of school. Suddenly, as he was jogging, the screeching tires of the van could be heard, making him run even faster to the school that was now less than half a block away from. He ran up the school steps and pulled on the door, thinking he had escaped the killer, only to be locked out. That's when he noticed the delay sign on the door. The sound of the tires coming to a halt also sent fear through him, making him look back at the van and the look in this crazy person's eyes.

"No, no, no, leave me alone," the young boy said, banging on the door, seeing the school janitor walking the hall. He ignored the banging, since the kid wasn't the first of many families that had come, unaware of the delay.

Now realizing he wasn't going to get any help, the young boy came off the school steps fast, sprinting in the direction he had just come from, four blocks away from his house. His heart thumped and his legs took long strides as his feet pressed into the concrete, thrusting him forward. His sudden burst of speed caught the killer off guard, making them get back into the van, shifting the gear into reverse, wanting to catch this kid, having come this far. They mashed the gas, steering the van, not to crash into parked cars.

"You're not going to get me," the young boy said, running hard and fast.

"Where do you think you're going, you little fucker?" the killer questioned as if the kid could hear them.

"You have to come with me, so stop fucking running." The boy briefly looked back, seeing the van closing in on him. At the same time, his foot caught a raised pavement, sending him flipping forward, falling to the ground as hard as he was running. In fear of capture, he bounced up quickly, running, feeling his book bag was weighing him down, so he let it slide off his shoulder.

Right then, his speed picked up faster than before, dropping the ten-plus pounds of extra weight in the book bag. Now a block and a half from his house, he started yelling out in fear to his mother. "Mom! Mommy! Help me!" he yelled at the top of his lungs. His mom's keen sense of hearing and motherly instinct of something going wrong with her child, made her come quickly to the door. The killer, seeing the screen door open, came to a halt, stopping the van and shifting it into drive, and took off to evade capture or confrontation. The young boy ran up to his mom, who came off the porch greeting him, seeing the fear in his eyes. She briefly scanned the area and saw the van racing off.

"It's going to be okay, baby. I'm going to call your dad and get him over here. I'm not playing this shit, trying to mess with mine," she said, still looking at the van until it turned the corner, vanishing. "Terrance did you get a good look at who was driving the van?" she asked her son.

"Not really, I was focused on getting away from them," he responded as they entered the house to call his dad and the cops. "I dropped my book bag trying to get away." It was a gift from his dad.

"Let me call your dad and the cops, and then we'll go get it," she said, caressing her son's head and comforting him while calming her nerves, thinking she was all too close to losing her child.

TWENTY

It didn't take long before the Harrisburg Police arrived at Terrance Johnson's home to meet with his parents, Jake and Mary. Each gave details on what had taken place up until his mother came out of the house. Terrance was a brown-skinned kid with brown eyes, his hair freshly braided in a design done by his mother.

Detective Anderson and Tores were also present with the uniformed officers, wanting detail, to help close this case. They were also surprised that this suspected killer would even try something like this with units doing a patrol around the neighborhood and school. Terrance sat on the couch eating a snack his mom gave to him, to calm him as he was speaking with the officers.

"Do you remember the color of the van?" Detective Anderson asked.

"Blue. I think it was a Chrysler," Mary responded, having stared the vehicle down, trying to seeing if she could get a good look at the driver.

"Can you tell us what kind it was?"

"Town and Country, I believe."

Detective Anderson nodded to the uniformed officers so they could look into this.

"Mom, don't forget they had a baseball hat, shades, and gray hair," Terrance blurred out as images of the person chasing him entered his mind. "They look white," he added.

At the sound of a white face, they feared a white male was killing young black kids. This would not be a good thing for the reporters to get a hold of, or for his family to spread on social media. The city would be in an uproar, terrorizing any white person they didn't think belonged in the city, even those from the city.

"Are you sure it was a white person?" Detective Tores asked, wanting to be certain.

Terrance paused, staring off, processing the image of this person's description from when they stepped out of the van. "It's weird, their face was white, but their arms were black."

"It could be makeup or a skin pigmentation," Detective Tores said.

"Whatever it is they have, I'm a bust a cap in they ass they come around again," Jake said, being protective of his son.

"Rightfully so, but we can't have that," Detective Anderson responded. "We don't need more homicides making our job harder."

"That muthafucka killing kids; they need to be tortured and killed."

"Mr. Johnson, we understand how you feel more than anything. Your son, thank God, got away. Now we need to find out details that will help us track this scum," Detective Tores said, wanting to bring calm to him and not wanting him to start shooting at every blue minivan he comes across.

"Terrance, is there anything else that you can remember that would help us get the bad guy?" Detective Tores questioned in a soft tone.

"Yeah, I hope y'all catch that person for what they did to my friends Michael and Ivan."

Hearing him say this made their hearts jump, and their minds tweaked to know the connection between the killer and these kids that knew each other. "Wait, you mean Michael and Ivan that were found dead?" Detective Tores asked in slight disbelief.

"Yeah, that's fucked up what happened to them."

"Watch your mouth, boy, you ain't grown," Mary said, slapping Terrance upside his head for his vulgar language. The detectives understood her motherly discipline.

"Who else do you hang out with?" Detective Anderson wanted to know, in case they were being targeted. Knowing that they were friends didn't make these killings as they originally thought. Someone was set out to get these kids, but who? He was wanting to know.

"It was five of us, me, Ivan, Michael, Floyd, and James. They tried to get me, but I was too fast," he said, drinking his soda, leaning back on the couch.

"Who did y'all piss off for them want to do this stupid shit?" Mary asked, standing with her hands on her hips.

"We ain't do nothing, Mom."

"Lying will get your ass whipped, boy. Tell the truth," Jake said, looking on at his son. He also wanted to know if he knew this person, so he could go after them on his own, making them pay for their attempt on his son's life.

"I'm not lying. We didn't do nothing."

"We need their names, Terrance, so we can make their parents aware of this information, so they can keep close tabs on them," Detective Tores said.

Mary chimed in, giving the detectives the information, "James Douglas, his mother is Elaine Douglas, a young girl about twenty-six years old, light-skinned, pretty little thing. Her son's cute too. Floyd Davis, his mom is Cordelia. She's a teacher at their school. They live on Twentieth and Market Street." They jotted down all of the information and suggesting that they keep their son home until this blew over.

"We're going to look into these names and see if they have more information that will connect the dots pointing us in the direction to catch this sick son of a bitch," Detective Anderson said, standing to leave, when an abrupt knock came across the screen door. Mary went to the front door and saw the dirty crackhead, wearing clothing that he'd had on for a week straight. His lips were white and chapped. His eyes were bulging, backed by this grin showing what yellow teeth he had left.

"What the hell you want?" Mary asked. Jake also approached the door, ready to remove the gun he had tucked under his T-shirt. The crackhead extended his hand with a white paper, scratching his head, unable to stay still.

"Um, this note is for you," he said. At the sound of "note," it alerted both detectives that were standing back preparing to exit. Soon as the crackhead looked to the side of Mary and Jake and saw the two detectives, he let the note go and took off running.

"This is some bullshit," JR said, taking off behind the crackhead.

"Stop chasing me, man. I'm just the messenger," the fiend yelled out, seeing the fast-approaching detective. JR closed in on him fast, diving and tackling him hard. "Aagh! You gonna kill a playa, tackling me like that."

"What the fuck you run for? You a got muthafucka killing and kidnapping kids and you want to be on this shit. I could have shot your bitch ass!" JR snapped, breathing heavily.

"Somebody paid me to give this note to y'all," the fiend said.

Detective Anderson picked him up from the ground and slammed him up against a parked Hummer truck. "What's that person look like, and how much did they pay you?" he asked, staring into the crackhead's wide eyes.

"They gave me a big-ass rock the size of a gumdrop. Beam me up, Scotty," he said, high and excited, thinking about getting even higher once the detective was done with him.

"Oh you think this shit is funny? We have two dead kids, and this muthafucka you say gave you a note tried to snatch the kid inside that house. Now what does this piece of shit look like?" Detective Anderson said, tightening his grip on the fiend, sending fear through him as he gave off the dark stare, meaning business.

"I was focused on the rock, but this muthafucka was looking real weird. Their skin was like patches and shit, face one color, arms another. I thought I was super high seeing this shit. They was real creepy, talking extra low. I did what they asked, wanting to get high man. I didn't do anything wrong."

"What kind of car did they have?"

"They was in one of those Uber whips, but they was driving. Can you let me go? You blowing my high. I need to get it back."

His answer let JR know they had probably stolen the car, and the van the kid said he saw them in.

"You think shit ain't real, huh!" Detective Anderson said, going into the fiend's pockets and taking out the package of drugs and glass stem he smoked the crack out of. He stomped the stem and the crack. "Now get the fuck out of here before I lock your as up." He let the fiend go as he went back to the house.

Janelle handed him the note, which read: "I will never regret my wrongs."

"Somebody isn't showing remorse for their actions." Detective Tores said, before walking to their car to process the case. JR's cell phone sounded off; it's Captain Jones.

"Anderson."

"I need you two in my office now; it can't wait until later," he said, hanging up.

TWENTY-ONE

The killer was pissed off that the speedy and fast-thinking Terrance had gotten away from them. This wasn't what they had expected or planned. Now they have to improvise this preplanned massacre of children, which would shock the city. They made it back to their house, where they sat in silence for some time, staring at photos of the dead Michael and Ivan. They enjoyed the Kodak moments of murder, displaying their craft as art, being a murderer. They even managed a sadistic smile reliving the kills of each victim, feeling a sense of self-gratification.

"Your friend got away for now. I'll get him, and he won't be so fast to slip away. Don't worry, he'll be joining you two soon," the killer said, speaking to the photos in that creepy low tone. This person wasn't always this way. Something made them snap, going over the edge of delusion, creating their own reality that made sense to them while justifying their means to kill.

They stood, putting the pictures away before heading upstairs to prepare for the next kill, to shock the city and the good detectives chasing behind them. Upstairs was also where all of the disguises were, in the bathroom. They entered, choosing their look of deception. They even had pictures of different people they wanted to look like that would help them throw off the detectives if they ever got a description of them.

"By the time they figure out it's me, I'll be long gone. I could stand right beside the good detectives in this new disguise, and they would never know it's me," the killer said, staring at themselves in the mirror. Their attention shifted, hearing a knock coming across their door. "Who is it? Do you want to die? Or did they figure me out?" the killer was thinking, staring out of the bathroom while standing silence, listening in for another knock across the door. They started laughing, realizing the knocking they heard had come from the neighbor's house. "Just when I thought it was about to get exciting," they said, getting ready for the next kill.

TWENTY-TWO

11:17 AM

Harrisburg Police Station

JR and Janelle were waking into the captain's office, noticing that he was in the company of someone they'd never seen before. Captain Jones stood from his desk to make the formal introduction. "Detectives Tores and Anderson, meet FBI specialist Angelica Mackie. She's a profiler out of Washington, here to assist with this case before it escalates beyond our control."

"We didn't need any help, Anderson, and I have this under control," Janelle said, clearly offended by her superior's decision.

"Detective Tores, having Agent Mackie here is a plus not a negative. Besides, this came from Mayor Jenkins, who brought the heat down on the chief."

Angelica stood five foot eight, with white-blonde hair pulled back, a light bronze tan, and sparkling gray eyes, looking fit, displaying her presence at the gym in between her time away from working. Her ability to do her job could easily be overlooked by her beauty. However, her credentials spoke volumes, closing dozens of unsolved federal and state cases. Outside of work, she was outgoing and exciting to be around with her sense of humor and welcoming personality. On the job, she was serious and focused. Angelica extended her hand to shake the detective's, sensing the slight tension with her unexpected presence, making the detectives feel as if she was infringing upon their territory.

"Easy, guys, I'm on your side. I want to capture this pernicious individual as much as you do," Angelica said.

"She's right, you two. We don't have time for turf wars when we have a lunatic running wild out there," Captain Jones said. They shook her hand, bringing ease to the room and one another.

"Speaking of lunatic, we just came from a call where our suspected killer attempted to snatch up a kid that was walking to school," Detective Tores said.

"To add what my partner is speaking on, we have a description of the suspect. Both witnesses stating the face was white with the arms being black."

"So you're telling me two different people came in contact with our suspect? Outside of the kid, who's the other person?" Captain Jones asked.

"Some crackhead," Detective Tores said, removing the note. "He was given drugs to deliver this note."

"That's the third note altogether. The first two notes were found on the dead bodies. This one was delivered since they couldn't get the kid," Detective Anderson said.

This also allowed Agent Mackie to process the mindset and behavior of the killer with being persistent in assuring a note was left behind, dead or alive. Captain Jones viewed the note before handing it over to Agent

Mackie. "What do you think of this?" Captain Jones asked her.

"I would have to get a look at the previous notes to get a full assessment. However, in my experience, when notes are left behind, they're usually the killer being expressive about what made them get to the point they're at, or simply a road map that will eventually track them down."

"I remember the notes, Agent Mackie," Detective Toes said, having a good memory. "The first stated: 'I will never be bad again.' The other said, 'I will never do what I did again.'" Agent Mackie recalled the words she just heard along with looking on at the note. She flashed back to her days in school, having to write in sequence on the chalkboard as the teacher's way of disciplining them for mishaps in class.

"I believe the person we're looking for is a school teacher or an employee of the school," Agent Mackie said, then added, "Have there been any problems with school teachers or employees at the school where the victims were found?"

"I had detectives check on that. They didn't say anything stood out to them," Captain Jones responded.

"One other thing we discovered today, sir," Detective Tores said. "The first two victims and the Johnson kid are all friends." Hearing this alerted the captain; at the same time, Agent Mackie's mind was assessing what she was hearing.

"From what I've learned thus far, the killer may still have the Jackson kid alive or dead, holding him as a trophy where they can revisit the moment it all started," Agent Mackie said before pausing to process her thoughts. "I would like to see the behavior reports on these kids. Something they may have said or done triggered the killer. It could be an employee they repeatedly taunted, angering them. Maybe a parent of a bullied child, or a teacher that snapped? So many plausible scenarios that make sense. However, we don't want to be deceived by narrowing our options, excluding someone who has no association with the school, especially if these kids hung out after school. Who knows what they got into or who they pissed off?" She looked down at the note once more before adding, "The first two kids must have trusted the killer, luring them in."

"Hold on, Agent Mackie. You're telling me it could be an officer or a public figure?" Captain Jones asked.

"I don't want to exclude that possibility. However, I'm leaning toward in and/or around the school area, which seems to be where these kids hang out," she responded.

"Captain Jones, Agent Mackie, we need to get back out there in the field to check into these scenarios you mentioned," Detective Anderson said. "Agent Mackie will ride with you two. Anything she needs, give it to her."

They all stood, preparing to leave. At the same time, the desk phone sounded off. Captain Jones answered as they started exiting. "Hold up, Detectives," he said with his index finger up. Something was wrong. Each of them could see it all over his face. He hung up the phone, seeming upset. "That was the Highland Park Police Department in Camp Hill. They said a ten-year-old kid was found dead on the Highland Park Elementary school grounds. Jack Gingrich is the homicide detective over there when you arrive on the scene."

"A copycat or they're trying to misdirect us," Agent Mackie said, fearing two killers could be on the loose.

TWENTY-THREE

Fifteen minutes later, the detectives and Agent Mackie pulled up on the crowded crime scene, no thanks to social media postings. With this area being predominantly white, with homes ranging from a quarter million and up, it made Agent Mackie think about the killer's change in MO, meaning the location outside of the group of young boys they had targeted thus far. They approached the yellow tape with their credentials out, so they could get through the nosey people standing around with their phones in hand.

"Get out the way before I arrest all y'all for obstructing this investigation!" Detective Anderson yelled out, getting his point across and scaring some of the people with his presence and threats of jail.

"Detectives, over here," Jack Gingrich called out, getting their attention. Jack was a short, stocky-built guy, standing five nine,

casually dressed with his dark shades, thick mustache, and strong, deep voice, a by-the-book detective.

"This is my partner, Tores, and Agent Mackie. I'm Detective Anderson."

"Good meeting you all considering the circumstances. Follow me over here, so you can see what we have. You can then tell me if it's connected to your case. You know this type of thing doesn't happen around here," Jack said before coming up on the crime scene specialist, Bobby. "Show these guys what you have, Bobby."

He did just that, taking a sample he had collected from his kit. "We have makeup transfer right here that I lifted from the boy's shirt and cheek. This is a blond strand of hair. Now as you can see the boy lying here is blonde but cut short. This hair is an easy ten inches in length."

"If the hair is synthetic, then it may be the MO of our killer," Detective Tores said. "I'll know for certain once I process it at the lab. Now here's the note that was left behind. I did dust it for prints, but there's barely a partial on it. I still can run it to see what we come back with," he said, handing the note to Detective Anderson.

He read it before handing it to Agent Mackie, who read it aloud. "I am and always will be. If not, then pray for me." Agent Mackie got a slight chill down her spine, thinking that there may be a copycat serial killer on the loose, since this note didn't fit with the others, not unless it was a misdirection to deceive her and the detectives. "From what I assess, if there isn't a copycat, then our suspect is becoming reckless diverting from their original plans, especially with the botched kidnapping earlier."

"Agent Mackie, I can't have a copycat running around here," Jack said as if he had a choice in his privileged community.

"Being financially inclined doesn't exclude you or this neighborhood from crime, Detective," Detective Tores said, sensing him feeling entitled.

"How did this kid meet his demise?" Agent Mackie questioned.

"So far, visually, I noticed redness around the neck where it looks like an injection from a needle. I'll know more once back at the lab."

"When your guy gets more info, get back to us. Right now, we need to work our side of the river. We'll keep you updated as we expect the same from you if anything else comes up that can help close these cases," Detective Anderson said.

"No problem. I just hope this is the only line we have to deal with over here. This community isn't ready for this type of shit," Jack responded.

"No one is ever ready. We just have to be professional and deal with it," Detective Tores chimed in, glad her partner didn't act like this guy. As they were leaving, reporters tossed questions through the air. At the same time, the others were standing around recording with their phones.

"I'm federal agent Angelica Mackie. I'm a profiler that will assist in closing this case. We're looking for someone who is a community figure, someone these kids trust. It could be the person beside you." Hearing her say this, everyone in the crowd started looking around at the people around them they didn't know, not realizing the killer was amongst them, blending in like a part of the neighborhood. They stuck around, wanting to know what they knew. They also thought Agent Mackie was a pretty little thing.

"Agent Mackie, is this child here a part of the Harrisburg murders?"

"We have to gather all of the evidence before we can make that conclusion."

"Is the killer black or Hispanic?"

"I got this one," Detective Anderson said, offended by the race question. "The race of the suspect has not been determined. It could be you, since you were among us, as Agent Mackie said. The color of the killer doesn't make what they're doing right. Statistically speaking, there are more white serial killers than any other race. Google that to confirm, before you ask any other race-related questions."

"Sorry if I offended you, Detective. I'm just doing my job," the reporter said.

"No offense taken. I was also doing my job getting the facts in order," he responded, tugging on Agent Mackie's sleeve. "We're done here; we have a murderer to catch." They headed back to the car, knowing they needed to get ahead of this killer that was killing as they pleased.

TWENTY-FOUR

The killer was watching the detectives in the car, wanting to blow them up to end the chase and investigation. The killer followed two vehicles behind the detectives in their stolen car as they drove up the ramp leading to Interstate 83 heading back to the city. The cars in front of the killer sped up, giving them a clear view of the detectives and their lady profiler friend, who was sitting in the back seat. They could even see Tores turning around to speak with Agent Mackie.

"What are you two bitches, I mean ladies, talking about? I'll deceive her too," the killer spoke in the low, sadistic tone. "I could make your son next, Detective Tores. Then it would really be interesting." The killer was so focused on their soliloquy, they didn't notice that JR saw that this car behind them had been following them since the exit. Agent Mackie, seeing the look in JR's eyes, checked the rearview mirror to try to get a better view of the person tailing them. He switched lanes. The killer did, too, wanting to stay behind them, not realizing. He switched lanes to get a visual.

"Detective Anderson, is everything okay?" Agent Mackie asked.

"I noticed this car following us since we left. It could be a reporter, or me just being on high alert."

Detective Tores was now looking forward as a bad vibe came over her, flashing back to a year ago, when they were working a case investigating a homicide. This drug kingpin sent his goons their way to silence them, to no avail. That night happened so fast, with them trying to evade the trap of two cars gunning for them. Janelle removed her sidearm, looking out her mirror to see the car following them.

"Change lanes. If they follow, I'll put a bullet in the tires to stop them, so we can close in on them, to find out who they are and what they want," Tores said. Agent Mackie also removed her weapon in preparation for what was to come. JR switched lanes. The killer flipped their turn signal on to switch lanes, however, holding their position, getting this feeling that something was about to go wrong.

"Oh, you almost got me to fall for it. I see you're onto me. Uh oh, it's time to go into character to fit this look I have. Why are you slowing down, dumbass? Oh, you want to get a close-up of me, huh?" the killer said, looking forward, knowing they were going to be staring intently to see if they recognized this person following them. Strange as it may be, they were getting a rush out of this moment, being so close to capture yet too far away for them to even know who they really were.

Agent Mackie caught the New York license plate. "The people from the big city drive crazy, fast, and up close on your bumper. I know from working a case in New York," Agent Mackie said.

"This isn't the big city. That shit could have gotten them gunned down," JR said.

"Now, back to the case, we need to look into those at the school and/or around the school that these kids trust and come in contact with," Agent Mackie said.

"They're either getting desperate, or trying to throw us off with this Camp Hill case, because he is not a friend with those other kids," Detective Tores said.

"Not unless they're friends on social media. We can look into all of this when questioning the other kids you guys say are the friends of the victims in the city," Agent Mackie said.

"Right now, if you ladies like, we can grab some food real quick on the go or sit down?"

"I'm hungry now, having skipped breakfast on my way in today," Agent Mackie responded.

"I got a good food spot we can go to." He started driving to the city.

TWENTY-FIVE

Janelle's mother, Margarita, was just getting back from her walk with her grandson, Pito. Pito was loving the bag of Swedish Fish candy his grandmother had gotten for him. He was cramming into his mouth, having no worries in the world other than how long it was going to take to finish the candy. Pito knew his mother would never give him the entire bag of candy, which was why he was cramming them into his mouth.

"You like the candy, Pito?" she asked.

His big innocent eyes stared back up at her. "Mmh hmm, esta bueno, abuela."

She laughed, taking her key out to unlock the front door. She noticed a large envelope sticking out of the mailbox, with no return address on it or name. This made her curious, so she hurried to open the door, so she could view the contents inside the envelope. Once inside the house, she sat Pito down in front of the TV, turning the cartoons on. She sat down on the couch across from him, preparing to tear the envelope open until the house phone sounded off. She leaned over, grabbed ahold of the cordless phone, and pressed the answer button. "Hole que tal? Quien es ese?"

"Cute little boy," a taunting morphed voice said, sounding like they were using a voice decoder.

"I could come for him now and you wouldn't be able to do anything about it." The phone call ended, sending fear through Margarita, making her tense up.

"Ahi Dios mio, por el amor de Dios!"

"Uh oh, que pasol, Abuela?" Pito asked what was wrong, even as a child sensing it in her tone and verbal expression.

"Nada, mi amor. Finish watching cartoons," she said, not wanting him to know grown-up business. She speed-dialed Janelle. Nothing, it went to voicemail. Her heart sank, not being able to reach her daughter. She got up, going into the kitchen and removing a butcher knife that she would not hesitate to use when it came to protecting her grandbaby. Once back into the living room, she called Janelle again. This time, she picked up. "Como esta, mi madre?" Janelle asked.

"Es malo, mi hija. Someone called disguising their voice saying they can take Pito and I can't do anything about it. I have a knife, mi hija. Nobody is going to touch my grandson." Hearing this, Janelle dropped her slice of pizza, sliding out of the booth, her heart thumping in fear of someone bringing harm to her mother or son.

"JR, Angelica, we have to go now. That pendejo called my house threatening my family." They followed without hesitation, also leaving their food behind, losing their appetites. "I'm on my way now, Ma. I'll call in units too."

Once outside, JR took the wheel, allowing Janelle to focus on the call with her mom and getting units out to her now. He flipped the sirens and lights on, mashing the gas. "This scum has really crossed the line fucking with your family. I definitely will turn my back when the time comes and you have to put a bullet in their face," Detective Anderson said.

"Most serial killers welcome suicide by cops. It's the easy way out," Agent Mackie said, understanding how each of them felt yet wanting to remain professional.

"I'll give that punta whatever they want messing with mi familia," Detective Tores stated.

"The fact this person has called your mother's place instead of yours leaves me to believe it may be someone close that knows your work schedule and whereabouts, along with your mother's info."

"Whoever it is will regret knowing any of this," she responded, angered, looking out the window, anxious to get to the house.

TWENTY-SIX

It didn't take long before JR turned down the streets where Janelle's mom lived. The tires screeched until they came to an abrupt halt, slamming his foot on the brakes, followed by shifting the gear into park. The doors came open, and each of them jumped out and ran up the steps to the house. Janelle sprinted faster, calling out to her mom. "Ma! Ma!"

Margarita, hearing her daughter calling out to her, opened the front door, displaying the fear on her face. "Mi hija, I didn't know what to do, so I grabbed this knife. I wasn't going to let them do to Pito what they did to the kids in the pictures," she said, pointing at the pictures in the envelope. The detectives and Agent Mackie looked over the photos, six in total, three of each boy.

Pito sat watching cartoons and finishing off the remains of the Swedish Fish, hoping his mom didn't stop him. Little did he know that was the least of her worries. She was glad he and her mother were okay. Janelle came over and kissed him on his sticky lips and cheek. At the same time, she caressed his hair lovingly, like a mother does.

"Agent Mackie, what do you think about this stunt our suspect pulled?" Detective Tores asked, coming over to her.

"They seem to be diverting from their original plan to misdirect our focus away from the intended targets. They're looking to shake things up while getting the opportunity to get their point across."

"We can have surveillance on your house around the clock just to be safe," detective Anderson said. "Safe is good, Detectives. Right now we need to focus on the remaining kids attached to the first two victims. They did something triggering our suspect to want bloody revenge," Agent Mackie stated.

"What if our suspect is a student?" Detective Tores asked.

"Or the parent of a kid that was bullied?" Detective Anderson added.

"At this point nothing or no one will be excluded. The intel we gather will allow my assessment to come full circle, bringing closure to this case," she responded.

"We need to go to the school to question the teachers and those who may have been directly affected by these kids, especially as these misfits, as the one mother called them, all hang out together," Detective Tores suggested.

"So are we going to eighty-six our list we spent hours gathering?" Detective Anderson questioned, not wanting to overlook the things that could help capture this scumbag.

"We'll go to go to David Percy's place first, then the school," Janelle responded. Shifting their attention, the house phone started ringing. Margarita's eyes widened in fear, knowing no one else called this home other than her daughter.

Janelle answered the phone in a confrontational way. "Who's this?" she let out, tapping her intercom button so the others could tune in. It was a morphed voice that sounded different than when Margarita heard it.

"So aggressive are we. Now you know what fear and helplessness feel like," the killer said, taunting Janelle at the said time her anger arose.

"Come here now, and I'll show you what fear and helplessness look like, when I kick your ass, before unloading the clip on you."

"Don't fuck with me, Detective, or I will bury everyone you love," the killer snapped back.

At the same time, Agent Mackie placed her hand on Janelle's shoulder to bring calm, so she could get something out of the call, knowing the killer didn't call just to argue, but for a reason.

"Now that I have your attention. I'm close, closer than you think. I will punish those who have sinned against me. When I'm done, I'll be long gone, as if I never existed." Click. The phone call ended, leaving them with that last thought. The room fell silent other than cartoons playing in the background.

"We have to go now. It's two o'clock, and the kids will be getting out in an hour. We have to make sure this list doesn't get completed," Detective Anderson said.

Agent Mackie was brainstorming, piecing it all together. “Our suspect has been at every crime scene, if they’re saying ‘closer than we think.’ Another thing they stated, you now know what fear and helplessness feel like. The only person that could feel this way is a student or parent. Someone that is being bullied or unable to fight their own battles. Not just physically but verbally, being harassed by these misfits as you called them,” Agent Mackie said.

“Closer than you think, they said, which means we need to talk to those at the school and keep our eyes open for anyone else that is closer than we think, like a police officer or someone who is at every crime scene,” Detective Tores expressed, reflecting back to the conversation and previous information gathered thus far.

“Not to change you guys’ plans of interviewing Mr. Percy, but I feel the school should be our next stop. Especially with this suspect acting rogue and desperate,” Agent Mackie suggested. They agreed, heading out after Janelle made sure her mother was secured with a squad car sitting on the house.

TWENTY-SEVEN

3:15 PM

The elementary school was being let out. The killer, as promised, was very close, ready to move in for the kill. They were inside of a stolen car they paid the thieves good money for. This allowed them to keep switching up, never leaving a trace. They sat back watching the good detectives and their FBI lady friend. Having them all here was going to make this even more exciting, kind of like a magician having an audience watching very close only to be deceived like blinking an eye. The detectives wouldn't even know it was them, even if they walked right up to them, since they were wearing another different disguise, with fake moles, thick eyebrows, a full beard from the kit, and even contacts changing their eye color. The cream they used also changed their complexion to misdirect anyone noticing their presence. The lightly tinted windows concealed them as they indulged in their McDonald's fries from earlier today; even now they savored the flavor.

"Detectives, are you hiding something from me? I know these boys should be coming out any moment now. I saw them go in. Oh, here they come. It's show time," the killer spoke in a barely audible tone. This killer idolized previous serial killers, studying how they planned each kill, up until they got caught. They, however, wouldn't make those same mistakes. Even if they got caught, it would be long after they got what they came for, in killing those who sinned against them. As Floyd Davis and his friend James Douglas were coming out of school, the killer was getting this uncontrollable urge to roll the window down and scream: "Yes, come to me now and it will all be over!" Instead, they pulled their vehicle out from their position, switching the hazard lights on. They even pulled up behind the detectives, noticing the sudden change in their movements.

"Oh no, this is not good. I'm not done just yet, Detectives." They prepared to pass the detectives' car when both of the doors opened, each of the detectives exiting along with Agent Mackie. The killer's mind went into overdrive, and at the same time their body temperature was rising, feeling the level of intensity with them now walking toward their car. The detectives made plans to use the kids as bait, allowing them to walk home together while they kept close tabs on them, not allowing them to leave their eyesight. This was why they exited their car, noticing someone looking to be out of place. Each of the detectives along with Agent Mackie had their side arms at the ready, moving in. The killer's nerves were sending waves of fear and adrenaline rushing through their bodies, forcing them to reach for their emergency backup—a 9mm Beretta, with one in the chamber, ready to fire.

"Detectives, please don't be naughty, making me kill you and this pretty bitch," they said before becoming silent as they came up close. They prepared for a burst of gunfire. They were a few feet away when the killer closed their eyes, taking a deep breath, exhaling, thinking to themselves, "I can't stop now. I have to finish what I started." When they opened their eyes, they could see the detectives and the FBI lady walking past the car heading to a minivan parked not far behind them. The killer took off, heading toward the two bad boys that needed to be punished while the detectives were distracted.

"Let me see your hands!" Detective Anderson said, aiming his gun at the Latino driver. Detective Tores got her weapon on the passenger. Agent Mackie covered the front windshield in case it got out of hand. The driver put his hands up, and that's when JR snatched the door open. "What you doing out here?" he asked the dark-skinned Dominican who was staring at him intently, before speaking in his deep Dominican accent.

"Last I checked, this is a free country. If you're doing a traffic stop, I have all of my needed credentials," he responded. The passenger looked like a true goon from the heart of the Dominica Republic.

"Oye estupido, if we want ID, we'll ask for it."

"I have the best lawyer in this city. I don't think he would be happy with your hospitality. Besides, Detective Tores, shouldn't you and your partner be chasing after the child killer that has this city ready to riot, instead of worrying about shit that's not related to homicide?" They were shocked he knew their names at first, but then it hit them that he'd probably seen their faces and names on television or social media. His words also triggered them to focus back on the case with the two young boys they were to keep close tabs on.

"Detectives, we are way off track. We have to focus on the boys. They're out of our sight now," Agent Mackie stated, fearing this was about to go wrong, having lost sight of the kids. They all rushed back to the car, driving off looking around trying to locate the kids.

~~~

The killer was driving down the street, pulling up alongside the young boys, ready to kill them and get it over with. They hit the switch, rolling the windows down. "Excuse me, can you tell me where Derry Street is? I got
~~~

lost." The two boys turned toward the voice, seeing this stranger. The killer sensed they were not going to bite the bait of being lost, so they held up a fifty-dollar bill. "I'll give each of you fifty dollars. I'm really in a hurry, if you can show me where Derry Street is."

Their eyes lit up at the sight of fifty dollars. They stopped in their tracks. "Okay, we'll show you, but give us the money first," the young boy said. Then he whispered to the other kid, "I'm a snatch the money, and we going to run."

TWENTY-EIGHT

The killer was getting that sensation again, ready to kill. They let their foot off the gas, and at the same time, sirens could be heard. They looked into the rearview mirror, seeing the detectives coming down the street. The killer was upset they couldn't get what they had come for. They allowed the car to drift before tapping the gas and continuing forward, leaving the two boys looking dumbfounded, wondering why they had driven off. "Goodbye for now. I'll be back when no one is expecting it," the killer said, turning the corner.

At the same time, the detectives pulled up, stopping the kids. "James, Floyd, come here. Did y'all see anyone that stood out as we discussed?" Detective Anderson asked.

"That car with the weird-looking old person that was about to give us fifty dollars to show them where Derry Street is," Floyd responded.

"They was about to get jacked for that money, 'cause I was going to snatch it and run," James stated, not realizing the magnitude of what was about to happen.

"Detectives, the money is the lure," Agent Mackie said, then added, "We need to get after that car before they get away."

Detective Tores directed the uniformed officers to secure the young boys, before jumping back into the car to chase behind their suspect.

They mashed the gas, racing to the end of the block, making a sharp right turn in the direction they had seen the car turn. The killer now had a one-minute jump start, with the detectives having stopped to speak with the kids.

"I wouldn't be surprised if we found that car abandoned. Our suspect has switched cars multiple times."

"Don't speak too soon, Agent Mackie," Detective Anderson said, seeing the burgundy Buick turning into the parking lot of Sorrento's Pizza. He turned the lights and siren off, closing in on this scum bag. The suspect parked the car, got out, and walked into the pizza place that was frequented by police officers. Detective Anderson pulled into the pizza parking lot quickly, right up beside where they saw this suspected killer get out.

"Tores, take the front door. Agent Mackie and I will hit the side door. Be careful," he said, racing up the steps with his gun out at his side not wanting to spook any kids eating in there with their parents. As soon as they entered, they scanned the area, seeing a few off-duty officers they knew, a few families and couples enjoying slices. They also noticed Officer Jefferson sitting eating a slice of pepperoni. However, they didn't see the person they saw entering this place.

"Did you see someone looking suspicious walking in here not even a minute ago?" Detective Anderson asked Officer Jefferson.

"I didn't pay much attention until you said something. They went straight into the bathroom," he responded. They all moved fast, closing in on the only bathroom in there, guns up at the ready. Tores came in the front door joining them, since they didn't see anyone exiting out the front door.

JR tried the door, and it was locked. He knocked, followed by announcing himself. "Harrisburg Police, come out now so we can speak with you," he said firmly. Nothing. No answer. The civilians inside the pizza spot had their phones out recording the detectives, suddenly breaching the bathroom door, only to be greeted with disappointment.

No one was inside the bathroom. This piece of shit had outsmarted them once more. How? They were all thinking. Detective Tores noticed the blue flannel balled up and stuffed into a trash can.

"They got out through the window right there like they had this planned all out," Detective Tores said.

"It also means they were here before, to even know about the window as a means of escape," Agent Mackie stated.

Officer Jefferson grabbed plastic gloves from the counter before joining the detectives to handle the evidence left behind. "Here you go, guys," Officer Jefferson said, passing gloves out to everyone.

Detective Tores pulled a receipt out of the top pocket of the flannel. It was from McDonald's. "This receipt is from the McDonald's in Highland Park," Tores said. "They did say they were closer than we expected. Which means they're watching our every move, making us steps behind them. What we can do is check with that location to see if they have the drive-thru photo with that time stamp. That will help us track this suspect," Agent Mackie suggested.

"Definitely run a read on the face mask they peeled off. The toupee too," Detective Anderson said.

"Don't forget the car outside. We can have that printed in case they slipped up. Especially with them being desperate, trying to take down the two kids at the same time. Our person doesn't fear the law. Look at how they came to the school area knowing it would be covered with uniforms and undercovers. Even using this place that is visited by police officers on duty and off. They're comfortable amongst the police," Agent Mackie expressed, having a strong feeling it could be someone in law enforcement, or just plain crazy, moving around and with no regard. Detectives Anderson and Tores each feared if it was one of their own, the city would riot, losing trust in those who were supposed to protect them. The city and country had been through so much with cops shooting and killing black people, let alone kids.

TWENTY-NINE

They exited the bathroom only to see people on their phones texting, tweeting, and recording them with evidence in hand of a killer that was once present. Detective Anderson's cell phone sounded off, and he ignored it, not wanting to answer it with the camera phones aimed at him recording every second.

"Tores, take the keys and drive so I can take this call. It's our guys on the other side of the bridge," he said, exiting the pizza place.

"Detective Anderson here. Tell me something good."

"Hey, Detective, I have news. You can determine whether it's good or bad. The hair and makeup come from a costume place. At first I ran a check on the makeup, seeing that it's different. I reached out to several stores around here. None of them stock this stuff. So I did a web check for costume deliveries in this area as well as Harrisburg. Philadelphia is the closest place. Here's the thing, the address is bogus."

"Bobby, get to the good news. I have a lot going on over here chasing behind this killer," Detective Anderson said, seeming to lose his patience.

"Okay, this is going to blow your mind. The names the costume and makeup were sent under: Janelle Tores and JR Anderson. My guess is someone is trying to screw you and your partner. Because if this got out, it would halt the investigation or at least pull you two from the case. It'll be the killer's way of slowing you down."

"This is some real bullshit, Bobby. Keep this under your hat so we can get ahead of it," JR said, ending the call and relaying the information to his partner and Agent Mackie. It also shocked him and the others how deep this killer was thinking ahead.

"With everything taking place so fast, there could be something at the beginning of this case we overlooked that could point to our suspect," Agent Mackie said. Her words triggered something in Detective Tores's mind, making her think about déjà vu. She made a sharp U-turn, heading back to the pizza place.

"What's running through your mind, Tores?" JR asked.

"Agent Mackie said we missed something. Think of the one person who has been at every crime scene. They are closer than we think? He was also conveniently eating a slice of pizza as we were chasing behind this killer. He also knows how good we are and that we'll eventually take him down," she responded, referring to Officer Jefferson.

"He was enjoying a slice of pizza, Tores, nothing else."

"Think back. He was holding a slice with no paper plate as they usually give with a slice. The table behind him had pizza on it, but no one was sitting there."

JR taking in her visual assessment, recalled the details he overlooked. They pulled back into the parking lot, ready to confront one of their own. This could go really bad if they were wrong about this assumption. As soon as they entered, they saw he was no longer present.

"I don't want to overreact, calling this officer out, and having it backfire on us," Detective Anderson said, not wanting it to be a fellow officer or waste valuable time that could be spent on tracking down the person killing kids.

"If it is him, it means he's the pendejo that called my mom, scaring the shit out of her. I could kill him for that and wouldn't lose any sleep, in or out of jail."

"Calm down. This is why I'm not all in on this idea. I do have your back, but let's think this through first."

"Detectives what we can do is pay him a surprise visit. He's not expecting us, so the advantage is ours," Agent Mackie suggested. They obliged, embracing this good idea.

"We should go now before any more kids end up dead or missing," Detective Tores said, having so many thoughts of Officer Jefferson betraying the blue uniform and shield he took an oath to uphold and honor.

THIRTY

The detectives drove to Penn Street in the uptown area of the city. What they noticed when pulling up to his house was the playground directly across the street. It was quite ironic with them tracking a child killer. The kids that were present at the playground were all running around. The others were playing baseball with a stick and rocks. Like a bullet crashing into a metal frame of a car, a rock hit by the makeshift baseball bat slammed into the detective's squad car, making them all alert, shifting their attention toward the kids, who stopped in mid-play seeing they struck a cop's car. When the car came to a stop, all the kids took off running, thinking they were going to be in trouble.

"Badass kids, playing baseball with rocks. They're wrong for that," Detective Tores said.

"Now we see firsthand what Officer Jefferson deals with daily," Agent Mackie stated as they exited the car and walked up the steps to Officer Jefferson's home. Each of them had a fifty-fifty split on him being the suspected killer. They just had to shut this lead down by speaking with him, so he could be excluded. The front door opened as each of them was thinking of their approach.

"Detectives what brings you to my home?"

"Unanswered questions, along with too many coincidences," Detective Anderson responded, sounding aggressive. Officer Jefferson's facial expression displayed his discomfort with their presence.

"Can we come in and ask you a few questions that would help us close this case!" Agent Mackie asked, bringing some calm back to the alarmed Officer Jefferson. He took a step back, gesturing them to come into his home, knowing he had nothing to hide. However, he was extremely offended by this. Especially how Detective Tores stared him down as she entered.

"Can I get any of you something to drink?" he asked.

"We can skip the hospitality experience and get straight to it," Detective Anderson said.

Officer Jefferson sat in the single chair facing them. "So what questions can I help you with?" he asked.

"Déjà vu brings us here. One thing I noticed coming in is those bad as kids. Now I get why you have a strong dislike for kids," Detective Tores stated, trying to subliminally accuse and associate him with the missing and murdered kids.

"What the hell are you talking about, Detective? I never expressed any dislike for children," he responded, offended by her allegations.

"She's talking about the convenience of you being at every crime scene," Detective Anderson said.

"That's my job. Check with dispatch. I work swing shifts on the hillside," he responded becoming angered. "Now I need a beer listening to this crap," he said, pulling a cigarette out, lighting it up, and taking a few long drags to calm his nerves.

Agent Mackie sat back, watching him puffing the cigarette while scanning the two detectives that thought he would even do something of this magnitude.

"You two will be hearing from my union rep about this bullshit. I'm not a child killer. You can check my home if you like, since you two will be out of a job after this stunt you're pulling, when you really should be tracking the son of a bitch that's terrorizing our city!" he snapped, taking another long pull on his cigarette, making the cherry flame illuminate as smoke filled his lungs to bring calm to him. "What about the Camp Hill kid? Was I there? Hell no, because that's not my beat!"

Right then, hearing his response, Detective Tores flashed back to the reporter she got into it with. They were at each crime scene. "Does it make them a killer?" she's thinking, knowing it's their job.

"I believe we have what we came for, Detectives. Sorry for this meeting, Officer Jefferson," Agent Mackie said.

"Sorry doesn't make this right. I'm an honorable officer of the law sworn to protect this city, and these clowns come in here disrespecting my honor. You'll hear from my union rep and superiors," he said, walking them to the door before slamming it close.

Once in the car Agent, Mackie gave the detectives her assessment on what had just unfolded. "We wasted time just now, with him. Our suspect is close as they stated. However, for us to assume it was this officer only means the level of misdirection is real, and we can't continue to go down this road, or we'll have a city of dead children."

"We had to have this talk with him. Otherwise, it would weigh on us, not knowing ," Detective Tores stated, feeling bad now for having confronted a fellow officer.

Detective Anderson's cell phone sounded off. Immediately he noticed it was Captain Jones. "I guess he called his union rep sooner than we expected," Detective Anderson said, answering the call. "Talk to me."

"I'll talk to you all right. What the hell is going on out there? I just got a call from the union rep informing me that you're questioning one of our own for this child murder beef? I didn't authorize this shit! And we sure as hell don't need the city thinking that it's one of us!" His voice seemed louder than usual, coming through the phone and getting his point across while making his presence felt.

"Sir, you know we're good at what we do. We only followed the evidence that pointed us in his direction. You can't tell me you want me to look away from the evidence, or this thing will never get solved."

"Whatever you and Tores do, don't fuck this up!" he said, hanging the phone up, leaving him with the thought of his last words.

"This muthafucka hung up on me again, not even giving me a chance to explain what we are doing out here. He wouldn't like it if I hung up on him. In fact, that's what I should do now: call him and hang up," Detective Anderson said, venting.

Janelle looked at her watch and saw it was past punchout time. "It's six-o-clock. I have someone to get home to. We can pick this up tomorrow, with a clear head," Detective Tores said, ready to see her son.

"One drink before you call it a night. You deserve it, Janelle," JR said.

"One drink and I'm gone."

THIRTY-ONE

A little over thirty minutes had passed by, and they were now all on their second drink, relaxing, enjoying the hot wings and each other's company. The conversation was far from work, more on one another's personal lives. JR found Angelica attractive outside of the workspace. Janelle, on the other hand, he always thought was sexy in her own way. However, she had a line she wasn't willing to cross with him, and he respected her decision 100 percent.

"You two have been partners for some time, and you resist this sexy chocolate hunk of a man?" Angelica asked Janelle, yet searching both of their eyes to see if they were holding back a secret of a heated night of passion they may have shared.

"We keep it professional, especially with the ME TOO movement in the workplaces. He is nice to look at, but my focus is my career and son," Janelle responded.

"What about now, like right now?" Angelica questioned, searching for her open door, so there wouldn't be any bad blood when it was time to work in the morning.

"He's a good-looking man, but like I said, my focus is my son. JR will be a catch for the one that can keep his attention," Janelle said, knowing he was a ladies' man, though respectable to the one he was with.

"So you won't mind me inviting him to Washington, DC, for dinner, or maybe a nightcap at my suite at the Hilton tonight," Angelica said, being forward and going after what she wanted. She didn't have time for long-term relationships with always being sent on cases in different states. The guy she usually chose would cheat on her, and she would always find out, so being emotionally involved wasn't really her thing anymore, especially when her ex messed around with her so-called best friend.

"You know he's a big boy, able to answer your questions directly. He and I only have a professional work relationship to solve murders," Janelle responded.

Angelica's eyes sparked under the lights, finding him sitting across from her. "Would you like to join me for a nightcap?"

"The pleasure is all mine. I think showing you the other side of the city would be memorable," he responded with a smile she welcomed, along with her thoughts of how this night was going to end. She didn't realize she was lightly biting her bottom lip. JR was thinking how she was a totally different person from this professional FBI profiler, and now this beautiful, erotic chick.

"I'll call an Uber so I won't be a hindrance to how this night ends," Janelle said sarcastically, seeming to catch feelings, something each of them picked up on.

"We'll see you in the morning, Janelle. Have a good night," Angelica said.

JR waved as he was sipping his Long Island Iced Tea. As soon as the Uber came and picked her up, JR and Angelica headed to her hotel suite, which was a few blocks away. It didn't take long before she closed in on his masculine frame inside of the elevator caressing his chest, raising on her toes kissing his lips, igniting that burst of passion, as if they'd known one another for some time, the flow of alcohol running through their body stimulating them even more. Her fingers found the buttons on his shirt, undoing it, parting the shirt and placing kisses on his flesh and toned six pack. Her hand pressed up against his manhood, wanting the full experience of it. The elevator door chimed and she paused. He tugged his shirt closed, in case people were standing outside of the elevator. No one in sight. She hurried out of the elevator toward her room. His eyes followed, turned on by this level of excitement she'd displayed thus far. Her body also lured him to follow fast behind her as she was switching. She stuck the door key in, opening the door, undressing from the front door to the bathroom. He followed her nude body into the shower, that became heated and steamy, with the dual shower heads spraying down on them, allowing him to truly appreciate the art of her beauty and body as the water raced over her flesh. His fingers and lips followed.

His fingers found her perfectly lined landing strip, parting her love before pressing his fingers inside and seeing how tight it was.

"Mmmmh," she let out, welcoming his touch. "Mmmmh, I want you inside of me," she said, softly wrapping her hands around his neck. He picked her up with ease, allowing her body to slide down on all of his thickness and length, filling her body up. "Oooh my, mmmmmh. Mmmmh, I like this. Mmmmmh," she moaned as he raised her up and down, taking her body for a ride of intimate, intense pleasure.

It was something she had neglected her body of for close to two years, after the heartbreak of her ex screwing her bestie. The steamy shower set the scene for this erotic session filled with her melodic moans, which stimulated his motion even more, thrusting deep into her love side to side.

"Mmmmh, mmmmh, JR. My body likes this, mmmmh." Her lips were up against his ear moaning, embracing the deep strokes that were creating a powerful surging sensation of orgasmic pleasure, pulsating, ready to escape her body. He could feel her vaginal walls contracting on him, making him thrust harder, faster, and deeper, reaching his powerful eruption, surging, at the same time she was moaning and releasing this powerful orgasm she'd been holding onto for so long. The melodic moans continued until they slowed, now kisses exchanged in between light giggles from her. How he made her body feel. His hands were still palming her soft bottom, spreading it, stimulating her even more.

"Let's finish up here so I can really take my time with your body," he said. They did just that, making their way to the bed, where round two started. As promised, more explosive and passionate, making her feel every emotion she'd felt for someone she'd been with for some time. The attention to sexual detail, using all of his gifts, opened her heart, mind, and body up to a side no one else would ever see. She didn't like to be vulnerable anymore; however, she was enjoying right now, until the morning came.

THIRTY-TWO

The morning hours came quick. JR and Angelica, lying asleep in the comfort of each other's bare warm flesh. Her head rested on his chest, her dreams of last night's passion. Neither of them realized they were past the normal work hours to wake up, especially JR, always getting up at five in the morning to start his workout and work day.

8:13 AM

The phone in the suite sounded off, followed by their cell phones ringing and waking them up, alert to what seemed like urgency with all the phones ringing. "Oh shit, Angelica, we should have been up," JR said, looking at the time and reaching for his phone that had stopped ringing.

She picked her phone up, half sleep yet coming around. "Hello."

"Agent Mackie, this is Captain Jones. We have a situation over at the school where the boys were left. I need you there now. Detective Tores is already on scene."

"I'm on my way now," she responded before hanging up, turning to JR and making him aware. "Something happened at the school, he needs us there yesterday from the sounds of his voice."

Each of them rushed to get dressed, unable to freshen up with another shower, only brushing their teeth with a hot rag and clearing their eyes from sleep. Angelica did put new clothes on, before spraying perfume over herself. Her hair was pulled back, not looking out of place. JR only tucked his shirt in, unlike it was yesterday, day hanging out. Besides, he didn't care, and the people on the crime scene wouldn't care either, so focused on what was taking place. As they were exiting the room, he tapped her ass lightly, flashing back to last night. She laughed, turning around and becoming serious. She leaned in as if to kiss him, but didn't.

"Last night was more than expected and appreciated. Now, right now, it's time to put your professional game face on because it is work hours, and we both have to be focused on one thing: solving this case," she said, getting his full attention yet him loving how she checked him, dividing work and play. It made him respect her even more.

With the lights and sirens on, it didn't take Detective Anderson and Agent Mackie long before they arrived on the screen. They saw the SWAT truck along with ambulances standing by, with dozens of police squad cars in the area. "This doesn't look like a homicide to me, especially with SWAT here," Detective Anderson said he was parking his car.

"It's a hostage situation from the looks of it," Agent Mackie quickly assessed. They exited the car, pushing past the crowd of onlookers, over to the SWAT truck, where they also greeted Detective Tores, who was being filled in on the details.

"Detective Tores, what's going on here?" Detective Anderson asked. She gave him a brief, slight look of disgust, seeing he was wearing the same clothes from yesterday. At least her freaky ass had enough sense and class to change clothes, Janelle was thinking.

"Glad you two could make it," Detective Tores said sarcastically, then added, "We have a hostage situation, with the child killer personally being present, to make a major statement and grand finale, so to speak."

Detective Anderson started to caress his bald head, stressing about the number of kids that may be inside and the likelihood of this person killing them all, especially after having come this far to barricade themselves in a place with no way out. "How many kids are inside, do we know? Are there any demands yet?" Detective Anderson asked.

"There probably won't be any demands. This is their platform, the stage they want to get their point across," Agent Mackie expressed.

"So far there haven't been any demands. The killer did make it known that they secured the rest of the school doors with chains. The principal over there said the front and back doors were secured to prevent the killer or kidnappers from coming in."

"This only means our suspect is from the faculty, as I previously made known. A teacher, even a janitor."

SWAT positioned their team around the school, having snipers on the roofs of houses and businesses, along with on top of the school in case they had to propel down. They tried to get a glimpse through their sniper rifles to look inside the classrooms, to no avail, with the killer having closed all the blinds inside. The killer also made them aware that there would be students standing by every window. This shut down all opportunities for flash bombs or breaching the window for entry.

"This crazy punta not only called the cops on themselves, but they also took one of the kid's phones, tweeting out what's taking place," Detective Tores said, angered by this situation along with the image of JR and Angelica flirting with one another. She knew how their night ended, and it didn't sit well with her. At the same time, she never welcomed him into her life. Now she wished differently, especially seeing the good sex glow all over Angelica's face, no matter how hard she was trying to be professional.

"Hey, Detectives, check this out," a SWAT member called out. They tuned into what he wanted them to see. A call coming from inside the school. It was the killer's direct line. "The hostage taker would like to speak with Detective Anderson."

He passed the phone that was on speaker while the SWAT member was recording it for later analysis or training. "This is Anderson speaking."

A deep, distorted, morphed voice came over the phone. "Glad you're able to make it, Detective. I have eighteen children, lives, that is, in this classroom, along with two teachers. Their fate is in your hands."

"What is it you need me to do to keep these people alive?" Detective Anderson asked, staring at the school, knowing this cowardly killer was held up inside terrorizing these kids and teachers.

"Listen, Floyd Davis is amongst the kids I have here. You can't save him. I want the one that got away, and his friend James Douglas."

"I'm listening, but do you hear this crazy shit you're saying?" he responded. The SWAT leader shook his head no to JR, so his hostility wouldn't affect the outcome of this hostage situation.

"Sacrifice, Detective, sacrifice. Two dead or the entire classroom full of students and teachers. The choice is yours; there will be no negotiating. You have less than an hour to figure it all out, or gunshots will ring out. Twenty to be exact." They hung up, leaving him with the thought and the impossible task he knew he could not fulfill legally or morally. At the same time, he was fully aware that *no* was a word he shouldn't use in a hostage negotiating situation.

"Look over at the mothers who have children stuck inside. This is a real-life nightmare and a mother's worst fear, of something happening to their child and they can't do anything about it," Detective Tores said, taking her hand through her long hair, feeling this intense level of stress while relating to what all these mothers were going through.

"Detectives, my guys are the best in the state. We'll do what we can to make sure the kids get out safe. The clock is ticking. Within the hour they'll be expecting to see one if not both of the kids they requested in exchange. We can't do that, so we have to strategically move in," the SWAT team leader said to the detectives before directing his men over the radio and ear coms.

"Detectives, what they're about to do could get all of those kids killed. Our suspect is mentally unstable, and scared by the events that led to this. They kill those kids, it will be a riot out here, and we can't afford it or be caught up in it," Agent Mackie expressed, showing great concern for this fast-moving case and crime scene with this crazed killer turned hostage taker.

"Sounds like you wish you two could have slept in?" Detective Tores said, taking a shot at them, with her sounding scared of an uproar.

"Last night was personal; this morning is business. However, I look forward to more nights with his excitement and passion," she responded, getting under Janelle's skin, making her face turn up and eyes roll at her and JR.

"Now back to business, shall we?"

THIRTY-THREE

"Detectives, we're trying to get cameras into the window. We have guys on the other side. They can see the kids in the other classrooms, but they can't leave with the doors being chained, so they're taking cover, not knowing exactly where the killer is inside. When my guys breach, they can get the kids in the other classrooms out," the SWAT team leader said.

"Just make sure those kids are out before your guys move in on the target. We don't want to give them more bodies to aim at," Detective Anderson said, feeling the stress of this standoff.

"I'm ahead of you, Detective. Remember, we train for this," he said before radioing in to his team, directing them.

Detective Anderson checked his watch, seeing how much time had slipped away, adding even more pressure since he was unable to produce the non-negotiable demands. "We need more time," JR said in a low tone, thinking about the young kids and their innocent lives that could be snatched in an instant to appease this mentally tormented killer. He made his way over to the worried-looking mothers and fathers standing on the other side of the yellow tape. "Everything is under control. Your kids will be coming out safe shortly. The SWAT team is the best in situations like this," he said, rubbing his bald head, trying to make the parents comfortable while stressing it all.

The eyes of the parents standing around shift to the right past the detective, seeing multiple children running out from the side of the school, having been set free by the SWAT team. The officer assisted the children, connecting them to their parents. The other parents stood by looking worried, realizing their children were still inside. The SWAT team remaining inside of the school was moving through the halls as trained in intense situations, ready to take down this hostage. The SWAT was also closing in on the roof, above the classroom where the kids and teachers were being held. The snipers aimed at the school also patiently awaited the shot.

The SWAT team was now outside of the classroom, preparing to take the microscopic camera and slide it under the door to see what was going on inside, so they knew exactly what approach to take upon entry. Nothing. The killer must have thought this out. They could only see the desk in front of the door. The other side of the desk was cloaked with a cloth, blocking all views of everyone's position. Inside the classroom, out of view, the killer was checking their watch, counting down the deadline time.

"You only have one minute and thirty seconds, assholes," the killer said in that low, sadistic tone, ready to start gunning down every child in this classroom one by one before putting a bullet in the teachers' faces. The students and teachers feared this, hearing the taunting whispers from the killer. They had the students and teachers standing facing the windows, so they could never get a look at them, even with the disguise. The killer, seeing time had expired, called to see if their demands had been met. Either way, they had a plan to make them all pay.

The phone inside of the SWAT truck sounded off, alerting those around, who dreaded this call, knowing they didn't fulfill the demands. The SWAT team leader held up a card for Detective Anderson that read: Stall Them Out. Buy More Time.

"Detective Anderson speaking. We have the kids coming now," he said, not realizing they understood what they were asking was next to impossible and against moral code and protocol.

"Failure is never an option, Detective. Especially when the stakes are this high. Now live with it!" As those words flowed from the killer's mouth, three rapid roaring rounds from a gun sounded off, echoing through the halls and immediately alerting the SWAT team outside of the room.

"Move! Move! Shots fired!" the SWAT member said, breaching the door. For Detective Anderson, it was like everything came to a halt as his mind tried to process and visualize these kids and teachers being gunned down.

Inside the school, the SWAT team had breached the room, guns out in front, sweeping the room. The kids in the classroom were screaming and crying out, in fear of being next or being gunned down in cold blood. After securing the room, the SWAT came over to the downed teachers and student covered in blood from the bullet wounds. The Davis kid was dead from a shot to the back of his head. The teacher who embraced the Davis kid also had a slug in the back of her head. The substitute teacher was bloody but still alive.

Both Detectives Tores and Anderson came rushing in along with other SWAT members, seeing the traumatized children. They could also see the substitute teacher not just saturated in blood, but with a gag in her mouth and bound. What shocked them is they knew this person. It was Brandi Jackson, the high school teacher and substitute teacher. This meant the killer targeted her, too, for making a public plea to track this scum down, and may still have her son. They removed the gag from her mouth, seeing she was trying to say something.

"He's getting away. He escaped long before you all came!" she let out.

As soon as she said that, a sniper outside of the school noticed someone exiting the back of the school, moving faster than normal. "Sniper one here. We have a runner exiting the back of the school. Am I green for the shot?"

"Take 'em down alive," the team leader said.

The sniper fired a round, racing through the air, tracking this fast sprinter and suspected psycho serial killer. The slug, just as recommended, was intended to halt all running, so it blasted through his hamstring, blowing out his thigh and dropping him in a forward stride. "Sniper one, targets down, ready to be secured." The detectives, Agent Mackie, and some SWAT members all raced to the back of the school, ready to confront this killer that had almost gotten away. The others escorted the children and Brandi Jackson outside to get medical attention and to be reunited with their families.

THIRTY-FOUR

"This son of a bitch almost got away," Detective Anderson said, running with the others through the back doors, seeing the downed suspect. The ambulance was also coming across the field since the sniper radioed in he had taken the suspect down. Each of the detectives recognized the suspect. It was the crackhead that had come to deliver the message at Johnson kid's house.

"This ain't right. This fiend-ass muthafucka ain't no child killer," Detective Anderson snapped. "Why was he running with this bag, containing a 9mm pistol, a wig, and a mask he looks like he freshly peeled off. We also have a school janitor uniform. I bet he doesn't even have a job here," the SWAT member said running down the list of evidence that was pointing at this guy. None of the detectives felt like this was closure. It just didn't fit his profile, with him being a crackhead.

JR got up in his face staring intently. “I know you ain’t the one that killed them kids, or those inside. Don’t take the fall for this, or allow this piece of shit to get away.”

“Man, I ain’t no killer. I just like to get high, and y’all fucked that up shooting me in my leg. This shit hurt like a muthafucka, man.”

“Tell us who gave you this bag and the crack to do this shit. If you don’t tell us, I’ll let you bleed out on this field, and you’ll die right here, no more getting high,” Detective Anderson stated firmly, pressing down on his wounded leg in need of resolve, in case the real killer was still inside the school or trying to get away. It didn’t help that the pain he inflicted was unbearable, making the crackhead faint.

“Really? I can’t believe this shit,” Detective Tores said.

“We need to get him to the hospital detectives. He won’t be going anywhere until we get all we need from him,” the SWAT member said, allowing the medics to haul him off. Detective Tores did get the bag the fiend was running with. They looked at the janitor jumpsuit, checking the pockets, feeling this wasn't over just yet.

Call it instincts, but as they came across a paper, the sight of it made their hearts race, confirming what they sensed. She unfolded the paper with a succinct note that read: THE GREATEST ILLUSION IS DECEPTION. POOF, JUST LIKE THAT, I'M GONE.

"The killer has to still be inside. No one else came out!" Agent Mackie expressed. They all turned, running back toward the school, hearts pounding, minds racing, guns out to take down this pernicious child killer. "Detectives, the greatest illusion is deception, because this killer masterminded everything, misdirecting us the entire time, making us look in one direction while they were standing close enough to deceive us," Agent Mackie said, breathing heavily from the sprint. Her factual assessment angered the detectives, having been duped by this killer, that had meticulously thought this all out. As they proceeded through the halls, they spotted a janitor standing six foot two. He was a white male, with dirty blond hair and a scruff beard, looking suspicious.

"Hey come here!" Detective Tores yelled out.

For some reason he took off running, seeing the detectives and SWAT. They closed in on him fast, dropping him with the taser. "Aaaagggh, you're hurting me!" he screamed out, feeling the surge of electricity rushing through his body.

"Stay down. Don't move!" the SWAT member yelled, with his gun aimed at the large man.

"What the hell did you run for?" Detective Anderson asked. Angered by them tasing him, the janitor stared at all of them with murderous eyes, not saying a word.

"You think this shit is a game? You want to be tough, huh? I don't think you understand the magnitude of why we're here. I will put a bullet in your face, and those worried parents outside will thank me for killing the scum that terrorized and murdered these kids," Detective Anderson said, waving everyone off. They all walked away, not wanting to be a part of what was next, if he opted to kill this man. Seeing the others walk away also put fear in the big man. "You going to let him kill me?"

"You killed those kids, didn't you?" Detective Tores tossed out there.

"I didn't kill no kids. What are you talking about?"

"Why did you try to run?" she asked.

"Okay, okay, it was Jerry."

"Who is Jerry?"

"The coke head. He used to work over at the high school. Then he came down here until getting high got the best of him and he got fired. The other day he snuck into the school, broke into my locker, and stole a jumpsuit. He said he would bring it back when I confronted him. He wouldn't do this by himself. He was on one of those new phones he can't afford. That's how I know he was doing this for someone. I ran because my name is on the jumpsuit. I don't want any problems, man."

"Detain him until we can prove otherwise not to," Detective Tores said. "Soon as crackpot comes around, we'll question him more, to see if he knows who is paying him in drugs or money. We find that person, it'll be our killer," Detective Anderson said.

"Let's just hope these two clowns weren't working together," Detective Tores responded.

"No, Detectives, we're looking for someone who is patient and calculated, to plan all of this out and get away thus far," Agent Mackie said, seeing these two men didn't fit the profile of being a strategic serial killer.

~~~

When the detectives, Agent Mackie, and SWAT exited the school, the crowd was roaring, thinking this large white man along with the crackhead that was recorded getting shot were the suspects. The news media outlets were also covering the story, wanting to know which of the two was the killer or if they were a duo.

"As you can see, America, the detectives along with SWAT are escorting someone from the school building. He could be the killer or accomplice to the one they brought out earlier. This city and its parents need these questions answered along with making sure these kids are safe," the reporter said before closing in on
~~~

the detectives to toss questions their way. "Detectives, is that man responsible for the child murders and events inside of the school today?"

"I'm not a fucking murderer, you douchebag!" the man said, hearing the question.

"Once we question both men, it will determine who is the one responsible for these murders," Detective Anderson responded.

"What about the Jackson kid? Are these men responsible for his abduction?"

"These men will also tell us what they know about this kidnapping as well," Detective Tores answered. They walked away from the reporters, knowing they would ask questions all day and night. They didn't have time for that. They needed to get to the bottom of this and fast, before the real killer, if it was not them, got away forever.

"Once we interrogate this bum, we can go to the hospital to question Jerry the crackhead." Detective Anderson said.

"My assessment, Detective, is that it wasn't these two. They may have answers that will point us in the right direction. That's if our killer was that careless," Agent Mackie said.

"It's always the smart ones that overlook the one thing that gets them caught. Something they didn't view as a problem or challenge, that would be in their way," Detective Tores stated, wanting to have full closure of this case that would allow her and this city to sleep in peace tonight.

THIRTY-FIVE

The news of the hostage situation at the school spread worldwide through the news outlets, Twitter, Instagram, Facebook live, and other social media platforms, increasing their likes and ratings for the best view and angles of this case. Down in Fredericksburg, Virginia, Dr. Derrick Kinue, a respected African, sat in his home looking at this breaking news, along with alerts on his phone, about these murdered kids and teacher, with one still missing. The doctor recognized Nicholas Jackson, the kid still missing. He was once a patient of his. Seeing the caption Still Missing under his face made the good doctor reach out to the Harrisburg Police Department.

As the phone rang, he muted the TV, wanting to make sure he was heard clearly when speaking with his accent. "Harrisburg Police hotline, how can I direct your call?"

"This is Dr. Kinue. I'm calling about the missing child I see on TV. I know where this kid is, and he is not missing no more."

"Hold on, sir. I'll put you through to the detectives working the case," the female operator said, sending his call to Captain Jones since he was the head of the department.

"Captain Jones here. This better not be a goddamn prank!"

"No, no, I don't think what I'm about to say is in any way funny. This kid Nicholas Jackson was a patient of mine. I treated him for his wounds."

"What wounds are you talking about? Where is the kid now?" Captain Jones asked, knowing there was blood at the crime scene. Could the doctor be talking about that? If not. What?

"The child was badly beaten by five young boys at his school. He was originally sent to Hershey Medical Center, where he was in a slight coma, before managing to come around. The mother brought him down here to live before he slipped back into a coma while asleep one night. After a CAT scan, we discovered damage to the frontal craniotomy and a hematoma, among other things. He died three weeks ago. The boy's mother is Brandi Jackson. She hasn't returned since the funeral."

"Jesus! Dead?" Captain Jones snapped, realizing what was going on. "I have officers out here searching for a dead kid thinking he's missing?" he expressed freely in no particular direction, just venting. "Send me a copy of the boy's Death Certificate now so I can have my officers close this out."

The doctor did just that, pulling the info up and sending it via photo. Captain Jones called Detectives Tores, and she picked up on the second ring.

"Tores, I need you and Anderson in my office now." They were already close by, so they came in a hurry, rushing to his office. "Whatever it is must be important from the sound of urgency in your voice," Detective Tores said, coming in with JR and Angelica.

"Don't sit down just yet. I got a call and a copy of this," he said, flipping the death certificate over before continuing, "The Jackson kid has been dead for three weeks." JR, Janelle, and Agent Mackie's eyes all widened as their minds immediately processed what he said and what it meant to their case.

"That bitch deceived us into thinking her son is missing," Detective Tores said, angered by it all, especially having felt sorry for her.

"She's our mastermind, no doubt about it, Detectives," Agent Mackie quickly pointed out. "She has the brains to manipulate these men into doing as she pleases."

"In case you two don't believe Agent Mackie's assessment. The boy died from blunt force trauma, by way of an ass whooping five kids at his school put on him," Captain Jones said.

"The five kids that were being targeted, she blames them for all her son's death and all the emotional and mental pain and anguish she's experiencing," Agent Mackie stated.

"I'll call the hospital now to see if she's still there," Detective Anderson said, making the call. It didn't take long to discover she was not there, because she was never injured, only covered in blood to look like she was a victim. "The greatest illusion is deception, and she played us all into believing she's the victim of a missing kid."

"Detective Anderson is right. However, we do have the advantage of her thinking she fooled us completely," Agent Mackie said. "I need you to go out to her house, where she'll go if she thinks she duped us. She has no worries of us coming or being arrested," Captain Jones said.

"Captain Jones, if she's not at her home, she may have fled back down to Virginia. It would be smart for us to fly out, getting ahead of her, assuming she's driving," Agent Mackie suggested.

"Move quick, and get her into custody, because she's not just a child killer, she's mentally and emotionally unstable, backed by being a scorned mother, making her even more dangerous to the public," Captain Jones said before excusing them, wanting to bring this all to an end.

THIRTY-SIX

5:02 PM

A group of federal agents were in position awaiting the go-ahead from agent Mackie to move in on Brandi Jackson. Detectives Tores and Anderson were in their positions staying low, ready to catch this sadistic killer for all she'd put them through. Now Detective Tores knew who was responsible for calling her house, taunting her mother with threats toward her son. A part of her wanted to beat her ass before slapping the cuffs on her. The reality was with the FBI present, that wouldn't be possible, because she would be in jail beside Brandi's crazy ass. Brandi hadn't arrived to her mother's house just yet. However, the Virginia State Police had been following her since she entered Fredericksburg. The lipstick-red G500 Benz truck she was driving with dark tinted windows stood out. She was also in the company of Nicholas's dad, Ricky Smith, who was released yesterday.

"Agent Mackie, this is Trooper Daniels. Your package should be arriving shortly."

"Thank you," she responded before directing everyone. "Any second now, everybody. Do not move in until the vehicle is parked and she's far enough away from it."

"Copy that."

Hearing this radio chatter got everyone's heart and mind racing, thinking about the multiple outcomes. The only outcome they sought was a calm arrest with no resistance. The agents hid in the bushes and behind cars and acted like they were going for walks, along with sitting in plain unmarked cars lying low out of sight.

"Everybody, eyes on. The package has arrived. Make it clean so we all can go home safe," Agent Mackie said, concealing herself close by Brandi's mother's split-level home with a two-car garage with enough space to park four cars.

They all anticipated that she would pull into the driveway, with only one car being present at the time. She didn't; she parked on the road, along the curb. She exited the truck looking like she had just come from a hot date, wearing six-inch pumps and white YSL jeans hugging her curves, flowing with the red silk, blouse adding to her look with her hair pulled back, a true beauty and mastermind, that was deadlier than one would think just taking a glimpse at her.

The agents were about to move in until the passenger door opened, followed by the back driver's side door, where two young boys exited. These kids must belong to Ricky from his other baby's mothers, the agents were thinking, at the same time not wanting to put them in harm's way. The smile on Brandi's face was like she had no worries in the world. She was even dressed like she was celebrating the child murders. Seeing this allowed the agents and detectives to see they were dealing with a diabolical individual.

"Move in, take her down," Agent Mackie said. Agents came out from all directions, even

inside of the house, having beat her there. They wanted to make sure the mother wouldn't warn Brandi of their presence.

"Put your fucking hands up now!" agents yelled out, closing in. She didn't flinch, or even have a swift reaction to run as most people would. She simply looked on at the agents, greeting them with her smile full of deception and evil.

"What seems to be the problem, Officers?" she asked, pretending not to know anything or why she was being closed in on.

"Brandi Jackson, you're under arrest for multiple counts of first-degree murder. You have the right to remain silent."

"I know my rights. I also know my name isn't Brandi Jackson. I'm not who you think I am," she said, trying to deceive the agents to no avail. They weren't buying her lies.

"I guess Nicholas Jackson isn't your son either?" Detective Tores asked.

"Correct, Detective, these are my children right here, Demitrius and Damien," she responded with a lost look in her eyes, as if trying to separate her world of lies from reality.

The reality was her real son, Nicholas, was no longer living.

"You're sicker than I thought, Brandi, Brenda, or whoever you want to be. You're going to jail for killing those kids," Detective Tores said. Brandi looked at Janelle, staring into her eyes hoping to make a motherly connection, to make her comprehend all she was feeling.

"Hey, Detective, those boys weren't so innocent. They hurt my baby, stomping him in the head over and over, all because he stepped on the one kid's brand-new Jordans by accident. Who does that? I couldn't even recognize my baby boy's face, it was so badly swollen. Unless you go through it, you will never understand my pain that unleashed the wrath to make those evil bastards pay for what they did to mine," Brandi said, becoming emotional, not even caring about jail. She did what she did for the sake of her son. The only regret she had was not being able to kill all five of those kids. Detective Tores did feel her pain. However, it didn't justify her actions.

"I'll never be able to know exactly what you feel. What you did, taking the law into your own hands, and playing God isn't justice. It's an injustice that caused even more mothers pain and anguish," Detective Tores said, nodding to the agents for them to take her away.

As they were walking Brandi to the car, she glanced over at Ricky with sad eyes, eyes that seemed to control him by way of manipulating him, forcing him to go for the agent's gun, in an attempt to break her free. Ricky got off one shot, hitting the agent in the chest before he was gunned down by multiple slugs from agents, the detectives, and state troopers that had him safely in their line of sight without jeopardizing the kids. Brandi stood watching with a sadistic smirk on her face before she was rushed aggressively into the backseat of the police car, to be transported back to Pennsylvania for full prosecution of the murders. giving the mothers and the city of Harrisburg closure.

THIRTY-SEVEN

Two months later, America, along with the city of Harrisburg, were still speaking about the child serial killer Brandi Jackson, who was on maximum security lockdown. Even so, many media outlets were trying to get interviews with her to pick her brain. Most of them were captivated by her beauty, seemingly overlooking the acts that got her placed in a jail cell. Brandi has also undergone multiple psychiatric evaluations to determine her state of mind to see if she's competent enough to stand trial. The detectives working the case, including Agent Mackie, all know this is a ploy and tactic of hers to try to deceive the system to get less time and to evade the death penalty, since these crimes were premeditated. Brandi was always thinking outside of the box and ahead, and even in her crazed mental state had a backup plan.

Detective Anderson and Agent Mackie had been in communication, keeping their sexual meetings exciting each time. He had also made his way to Washington to spend time with her, making her appreciate crossing his path. Janelle was spending more time with her mom and son, especially on her days off, making memories that allowed her to forget the long, hard days of working homicide.

7:16 PM

Detective Anderson was heading home after a long day of work on a new homicide case involving a love triangle. As he was driving home, he was on the phone with Angelica talking about their next date destination. "Baltimore is a good spot for seafood lovers like ourselves. I also saw online a nice hotel that sits overlooking the harbor. It's called the Renaissance. It also has a shopping gallery attached to it, so for added adventure we can get some sexy lingerie to take date night to another level, looking out at the yachts on the water," JR said in his sexy phone voice.

"I like that you're thoughtful, planning ahead and checking out destinations. Now I'm looking forward to this mini-vacation to Baltimore, to spend time and have fun with you and that sexy chocolate body," Angelica said in a soft, sensual tone, visualizing herself in this hotel suite overlooking the harbor. She searched the location as he was speaking, checking out the rooms, views, and reviews for the service and food.

"Once I get home, we can do a little Zoom date night with a little sexy time as you like to call it," JR said, making her laugh, reflecting back to other nights they did the Zoom video. JR came to a red light and stopped, ready to get home so he could see her on the screen in his place of comfort.

"What would you like me to wear tonight?" she asked. As he was preparing to respond, processing what he wanted her to wear, a white Yukon Denali truck came up beside his car in the other lane. Normally he wouldn't pay it any mind, until he recognized the face when the dark tinted windows rolled down. "Are you thinking that much about it?" she asked.

"Hold on, Angelica, someone I know just pulled up to the side of me."

"I told you, you greedy muthafucka, you would pay for stealing my money!" Before JR could react by removing his sidearm, an all-black minivan came around the side of the Yukon, blocking the front of his car. The side van door swung open, exposing two gunmen with AK-47s squeezing, unleashing over fifty rounds before driving off fast, leaving Detective Anderson slumped over, his car riddled with bullets. Angelica screamed in fear, hearing the roaring of gunfire, unable to do anything.

"JR! JR, answer me! I'll get you help, baby," she said, calling 911 and alerting them to his position. The hit was Lewis Lexiton's Dominican connect that supplied him with kilos of cocaine. Lewis told them what happened with the detective stealing the cocaine and money. He also showed them proof from the cameras he had inside and out of his house. Lewis was valuable to them and the cop meant nothing, so they made an example out of him.

THE WORLD'S NEW STORYTELLER

To order books, please fill out the order form below:
To order films please go to www.good2gofilms.com

Name:____
Address:____
City:__________State:_______Zip Code: _________
Phone:____
Email:____
Method of Payment: Check VISA MASTERCARD
Credit Card#:____
Name as it appears on card: _____________________________
Signature: ____

Item Name	Price	Qty	Amount
48 Hours to Die – Silk White	$14.99		
A Hustler's Dream – Ernest Morris	$14.99		
A Hustler's Dream 2 – Ernest Morris	$14.99		
A Thug's Devotion – J. L. Rose and J. M. McMillon	$14.99		
All Eyes on Tommy Gunz – Warren Holloway	$14.99		
Black Reign – Ernest Morris	$14.99		
Bloody Mayhem Down South – Trayvon Jackson	$14.99		
Bloody Mayhem Down South 2 – Trayvon Jackson	$14.99		
Business Is Business – Silk White	$14.99		
Business Is Business 2 – Silk White	$14.99		
Business Is Business 3 – Silk White	$14.99		
Cash In Cash Out – Assa Raymond Baker	$14.99		
Cash In Cash Out 2 – Assa Raymond Baker	$14.99		
Childhood Sweethearts – Jacob Spears	$14.99		
Childhood Sweethearts 2 – Jacob Spears	$14.99		
Childhood Sweethearts 3 – Jacob Spears	$14.99		
Childhood Sweethearts 4 – Jacob Spears	$14.99		
Connected To The Plug – Dwan Marquis Williams	$14.99		
Connected To The Plug 2 – Dwan Marquis Williams	$14.99		
Connected To The Plug 3 – Dwan Williams	$14.99		
Cost of Betrayal – Warren.C. Holloway	$14.99		
Cost of Betrayal 2 – Warren.C. Holloway	$14.99		
Deadly Reunion – Ernest Morris	$14.99		
Dream's Life – Assa Raymond Baker	$14.99		
Finding Her Love – Warren C. Holloway	$14.99		
Flipping Numbers – Ernest Morris	$14.99		
Flipping Numbers 2 – Ernest Morris	$14.99		

Forbidden Pleasure – Ernest Morris	$14.99		
He Loves Me, He Loves You Not – Mychea	$14.99		
He Loves Me, He Loves You Not 2 – Mychea	$14.99		
He Loves Me, He Loves You Not 3 – Mychea	$14.99		
He Loves Me, He Loves You Not 4 – Mychea	$14.99		
He Loves Me, He Loves You Not 5 – Mychea	$14.99		
Killing Signs – Ernest Morris	$14.99		
Killing Signs 2 – Ernest Morris	$14.99		
Kings of the Block – Dwan Willams	$14.99		
Kings of the Block 2 – Dwan Willams	$14.99		
Lord of My Land – Jay Morrison	$14.99		
Lost and Turned Out – Ernest Morris	$14.99		
Love & Dedication – Warren.C. Holloway	$14.99		
Love Hates Violence – De'Wayne Maris	$14.99		
Love Hates Violence 2 – De'Wayne Maris	$14.99		
Love Hates Violence 3 – De'Wayne Maris	$14.99		
Love Hates Violence 4 – De'Wayne Maris	$14.99		
Married To Da Streets – Silk White	$14.99		
M.E.R.C. – Make Every Rep Count Health and Fitness	$14.99		
Mercenary In Love – J.L. Rose & J.L. Turner	$14.99		
Money Make Me Cum – Ernest Morris	$14.99		
Murder And Deception – Warren C. Holloway	$14.99		
My Besties – Asia Hill	$14.99		
My Besties 2 – Asia Hill	$14.99		
My Besties 3 – Asia Hill	$14.99		
My Besties 4 – Asia Hill	$14.99		
My Boyfriend's Wife – Mychea	$14.99		
My Boyfriend's Wife 2 – Mychea	$14.99		
My Brothers Envy – J. L. Rose	$14.99		
My Brothers Envy 2 – J. L. Rose	$14.99		
Naughty Housewives – Ernest Morris	$14.99		
Naughty Housewives 2 – Ernest Morris	$14.99		
Naughty Housewives 3 – Ernest Morris	$14.99		
Naughty Housewives 4 – Ernest Morris	$14.99		

MURDER & DECEPTION

Never Be The Same – Silk White	$14.99		
Scarred Faces – Assa Raymond Baker	$14.99		
Scarred Knuckles – Assa Raymond Baker	$14.99		
Secrets in the Dark – Ernest Morris	$14.99		
Secrets in the Dark 2 – Ernest Morris	$14.99		
Shades of Revenge – Assa Raymond Baker	$14.99		
Slumped – Jason Brent	$14.99		
Someone's Gonna Get It – Mychea	$14.99		
Stranded – Silk White	$14.99		
Supreme & Justice – Ernest Morris	$14.99		
Supreme & Justice 2 – Ernest Morris	$14.99		
Supreme & Justice 3 – Ernest Morris	$14.99		
Tears of a Hustler – Silk White	$14.99		
Tears of a Hustler 2 – Silk White	$14.99		
Tears of a Hustler 3 – Silk White	$14.99		
Tears of a Hustler 4 – Silk White	$14.99		
Tears of a Hustler 5 – Silk White	$14.99		
Tears of a Hustler 6 – Silk White	$14.99		
The Betrayal Within – Ernest Morris	$14.99		
The Last Love Letter – Warren Holloway	$14.99		
The Last Love Letter 2 – Warren Holloway	$14.99		
The Panty Ripper – Reality Way	$14.99		
The Panty Ripper 3 – Reality Way	$14.99		
The Solution – Jay Morrison	$14.99		
The Teflon Queen – Silk White	$14.99		
The Teflon Queen 2 – Silk White	$14.99		
The Teflon Queen 3 – Silk White	$14.99		
The Teflon Queen 4 – Silk White	$14.99		
The Teflon Queen 5 – Silk White	$14.99		
The Teflon Queen 6 – Silk White	$14.99		
The Vacation – Silk White	$14.99		
The Webpage Murder – Ernest Morris	$14.99		
The Webpage Murder 2 – Ernest Morris	$14.99		
Tied To A Boss – J.L. Rose	$14.99		

Tied To A Boss 2 – J.L. Rose	$14.99		
Tied To A Boss 3 – J.L. Rose	$14.99		
Tied To A Boss 4 – J.L. Rose	$14.99		
Tied To A Boss 5 – J.L. Rose	$14.99		
Time Is Money – Silk White	$14.99		
Tomorrow's Not Promised – Robert Torres	$14.99		
Tomorrow's Not Promised 2 – Robert Torres	$14.99		
Two Mask One Heart – Jacob Spears and Trayvon Jackson	$14.99		
Two Mask One Heart 2 – Jacob Spears and Trayvon Jackson	$14.99		
Two Mask One Heart 3 – Jacob Spears and Trayvon Jackson	$14.99		
When Love Happens – Warren Holloway	$14.99		
Wife – Assa Ray Baker & Raneissa Baker	$14.99		
Wife 2 – Assa Ray Baker & Raneissa Baker	$14.99		
Wrong Place Wrong Time – Silk White	$14.99		
Young Goonz – Reality Way	$14.99		
Subtotal:			
Tax:			
Shipping (Free) U.S. Media Mail:			
Total:			

Make Checks Payable to Good2Go Publishing, 7311 W Glass Lane, Laveen, AZ 85339

CPSIA information can be obtained
at www.ICGtesting.com
Printed in the USA
LVHW020415240523
747814LV00009B/691